Only Eva

JUDI CURTIN grew up in Cork and now lives in Limerick where she is married with three children. Judi is the author of *Eva's Journey*, *Eva's Holiday*, *Leave it to Eva* and *Eva and the Hidden Notebook*, as well as the best-selling 'Alice & Megan' series. With Roisin Meaney, she is the author of *See If I Care*. She has also written three novels, *Sorry, Walter*, *From Claire to Here* and *Almost Perfect*. Her books have sold into Serbian, Portuguese, German, Russian, Lithuanian and most recently to Australia and New Zealand.

The 'Alice & Megan' series

Alice Next Door
Alice Again
Don't Ask Alice
Alice in the Middle
Bonjour Alice
Alice & Megan Forever
Alice to the Rescue
Viva Alice
Alice & Megan's Cookbook

The 'Eva' Series

Eva's Journey
Eva's Holiday
Leave it to Eva
Eva and the Hidden Diary

Other Books

See If I Care (with Roisin Meaney)

Judi Curtin

ONLY EVA

THE O'BRIEN PRESS
DUBLIN

First published 2015 by The O'Brien Press Ltd,
12 Terenure Road East, Rathgar, Dublin 6, Ireland.
Tel: +353 1 4923333; Fax: +353 1 4922777
E-mail: books@obrien.ie
Website: www.obrien.ie

ISBN: 978-1-84717-666-0

1 3 5 6 4 2
15 17 18 16

Layout and design: The O'Brien Press Ltd
Cover illustration: Woody Fox
Printed and bound by CPI Group (UK) Ltd, Croydon, CR0 4YY
The paper used in this book is produced using pulp from managed forests

For Mum and Dad

While I was struggling to find an idea for this book, Sheenagh Murphy told me a story about her granny that brought a tear to my eye. That night Gigi's story came to me – huge thanks to Sheenagh for the inspiration.

Thanks to my writing friends, Sarah Webb and Oisín McGann, who are a constant source of advice, encouragement and book titles.

Thanks to everyone at The O'Brien Press for their ongoing support. Special thanks to super-editor, Helen Carr.

Chapter One

'Homework is totally cruel and unfair. There should be a law against it.'

We were walking home from school, and I couldn't stop thinking about the history essay I had to write, and the two pages of totally impossible maths questions I had to solve.

Ella laughed. 'Why don't you leave your homework until later?'

'I might as well just get it over with – and anyway, what else have I got to do?'

'You could come with me.'

'Where are you going?' I asked, hoping she was going to say she was on her way to a supercool party or something.

'I'm going to visit my granny.'

Grannies are supposed to be grey and boring, but Ella's is really cool. Her name is Grace, but everyone calls her Gigi. She's got hair down to her shoulders, and she wears the weirdest clothes ever. Sometimes, when she goes out for a walk, people point at her and laugh, but Gigi doesn't care. She just laughs back, and then the other people end up looking kind of stupid. Gigi lives in a totally cool cottage near the park, and she's got the cutest dog I've ever seen.

'Great,' I said. 'I'd love to come with you. We can play with Pedro for a bit, and maybe we'll get lucky and Gigi will have made some of her totally delicious macaroons. Those passion fruit ones are the yummiest things I've ever, ever eaten.'

I was so busy imagining the soft, sweet macaroons dissolving on my tongue that it took me a minute to notice that Ella wasn't answering.

'Ell?'

I stopped walking when I saw that she had tears in her eyes.

'What is it?' I asked. 'What's wrong?'

'Everything,' she said, wiping her eyes with her coat sleeve. 'I didn't tell you before – I was too upset to talk about it.'

'Tell me what?'

'Gigi fell a few months ago, and since then she hasn't really been able to manage on her own. Last week she had go to live in a nursing home.'

'Maybe that's not so bad,' I said. 'My dad's aunt lived in a nursing home for years and she totally loved it. She even had a boyfriend for a bit – a weird old guy who wore odd socks and smelled like the inside of an ancient wardrobe. Dad's aunt said the nursing home was the best place she'd ever lived in her whole life.'

'That's sweet,' said Ella. 'And we thought Gigi was going to be happy in her nursing home too. She visited there with Mum and Dad a few weeks ago, and it seemed lovely. The head nurse was really gentle and kind, but she retired the day before Gigi moved in. And the new nurse ...'

'What about her?'

'She used to be a nurse in the army – and it shows. Her name is Nurse Fitch, but Gigi calls her Nurse Witch. She shouts a lot and bosses everyone around. She's brought in all these stupid rules and regulations – like she's running a jail and the old people are her prisoners.'

'Poor Gigi! That sounds awful. If things are that bad though, maybe she could move to another nursing home?'

'That wouldn't work. We want her to be nearby so we can visit a lot, and that means there isn't really a choice. Anyway, even if Gigi moved somewhere else, I still don't think she'd be properly happy. She misses everything about her old life. She misses being independent. She misses being able to bake, and mess around in her garden. She misses her old friends and neighbours.'

'But maybe she'll make new friends in the nursing home?'

'That's what Mum suggested, but Gigi said all the other nursing home residents are boring old farts.'

I giggled, glad to hear that Gigi hadn't lost all of her spark.

Ella didn't laugh with me though. 'I haven't told you the very worst thing. Most of all Gigi misses ...'

She stopped talking, and I could see that she was trying to hold back her tears again. Suddenly I understood.

'Pedro,' I whispered. 'What happened to Pedro?'

Ella blinked quickly, making her eyes look all big and watery.

'I miss him so much,' she said. 'We wanted him to come and live with us, but Dad's allergic to dogs, so that was never going to work.'

'So where is he?'

'He had to go to live with my cousins in Tipperary.'

'But that's *miles* away.'

'I know. We took him there last week, and watching Gigi saying goodbye to him was the saddest thing I've ever seen.'

Now tears came to my eyes too.

'Let's go,' I said. 'Granny-cheering-up is one of my many unrecognised talents.'

'I guess,' said Ella. 'Only thing is, Gigi will act happy when we're there, but I know that as soon as we leave, she'll be sad again. Unless—'

She stopped talking and grabbed my arm.

'Unless what?' I asked.

'You can help,' she said.

'How?'

'You can fix everything.'

'I'm not sure that—'

She interrupted me. 'Why didn't I think of this before? You're the expert helper-outer.'

'But—'

She ignored me. 'You fix things when no one else can.'

'I do?'

'Of course you do! When Ruby's mum couldn't get upstairs, you arranged for your dad to put in a stair-lift for her. When Kate's favourite tree was being cut down, you started the campaign that saved it. After you found Daisy's ancient old diary, you even managed to fix her problems that had happened nearly a hundred years ago – that was total genius. We could stand here for a week, talking about all the amazing things you've done.'

I could feel my face going red.

'All those things just sort of happened,' I said. 'And I didn't do any of them on my own. Heaps of people helped me.'

'It was mostly you, though. Face it, Eva, if anyone can help Gigi, it's you.'

'It's nice of you to say that,' I said. 'But I don't even know where to start. I don't know a single thing about nursing homes.'

'So why are we hanging around here?' asked Ella. 'Let's go and get started.'

Chapter Two

The nursing home was just around the corner from Ella's house, so it only took us a few minutes to get there.

We walked up the gravel drive and stopped at a big glass door. Ella keyed in a code, the door clicked open, and I followed her inside.

We were standing in a reception area. It was a bit like a hotel – except hotels don't usually have big lists of rules and regulations on every wall, and they don't smell like old, boiled cabbage.

A very cross-looking woman was sitting at a desk. She narrowed her eyes and stared at us like we were criminals who were planning to steal everything she'd ever owned.

'I'm guessing that's Nurse Witch?' I whispered, and Ella nodded.

'My friend and I are just going up to see Gigi,' said Ella. 'Is that OK?'

'Stand up tall when you're talking,' said Nurse Witch. 'You're slouched down like a sack of potatoes.'

I wanted to giggle, but I didn't dare. There was something seriously scary about this woman. Next to me, I could sense Ella standing up straighter.

'Two children together,' said Nurse Witch. 'I don't like that. I don't like that one little bit. Do try and behave yourselves. I don't want to hear that you've been running around and climbing on things.'

'We'll be good, we promise,' said Ella, and then she grabbed my arm and pulled me along the corridor.

'OMG,' I said. 'Does that woman think we're six?'

Ella rolled her eyes. 'I guess, but what's even worse is that she treats the old people like that too. She shouts orders at them all the time, like she thinks she's still in the army.'

'That's really mean.'

'I know – and most of her new rules are really mean too.'

'Like what?'

'Well, she's brought in a new bedtime rule, like she's Supernanny and the old people are badly-brought-up kids. She locks up the residents' lounges at eight o'clock, and everyone has to stay in their rooms after that, whether they want to or not. Gigi doesn't sleep that much, and she finds the nights very long and boring.'

We were passing a room that was crowded with old people, and I tried not to stare. The TV was on, but no one was looking at it.

Most people were just gazing into space. One woman waved madly, but when I waved back, she stuck her tongue out at me.

I followed Ella into the lift. 'I guess, in one way, Gigi's kind of lucky,' she said. 'Her room's upstairs.'

'Why's that lucky?' I asked. 'Isn't the smell of cabbage so bad up there?'

Ella giggled. 'The upstairs people don't get spied on *quite* so much. The sickest people, and the ones who might wander off, are all on the ground floor where Nurse Witch can keep a close eye on them. It's a bit like a teacher making the troublesome kids sit at the front of the class.'

By now the lift doors had pinged open and we were walking down a long corridor. Our feet didn't make a sound on the soft, mud-coloured carpet. Some of the doors were open, but I didn't dare look inside any of them. I told myself I was being polite, but really I was just afraid of what I might see.

Halfway along the corridor, Ella pushed open a door and we went inside.

Gigi was sitting in an armchair. She was wearing a purple ruffled skirt, a huge black jumper and a pair of hiking boots. I wanted to laugh, but I couldn't – Gigi was staring out the window and looking really sad.

'Hey, Gigi,' said Ella. 'It's me, and I've brought Eva to see you too.'

'Ella, darling. It's so nice to see you. And Eva – how sweet of you to come.'

As Gigi turned towards us, she gave one of the big smiles I remembered. A second later though, her smile had vanished completely, leaving me wondering if I had only imagined it.

After Gigi had given us both huge hugs, Ella and I sat on the bed, and Gigi asked us loads of questions about school and stuff.

'What about you, Gigi?' asked Ella in the end. 'Have you made any friends here yet?'

Gigi made a face. 'There's no one interesting here. Like I told your mother, they're all boring old fuddy-duddies.'

'But you don't know them yet,' said Ella. 'Maybe you need to give them a chance? Have you thought that maybe they think *you're* a boring old fuddy-duddy too?'

I looked at Gigi's long hair and weird clothes and decided that only a blind person could mistake her for a boring fuddy-duddy.

'So what do you do all day?' I asked, trying to change the subject.

'I sit here and wait for them to bring me cups of tea,' said Gigi.

'What do you mean?' I asked, remembering how the kettle in Gigi's house was always bubbling on the cooker. She spent half her time making endless cups of tea for her friends and neighbours.

Now Gigi looked like she was going to cry. 'Before I moved in to this awful place, there used to be a tea and coffee station in the lounge, and residents could help themselves to hot drinks and biscuits whenever they wanted. Nurse Witch got rid of it though. She said the biscuits were bad for us, and the hot water represented a health and safety risk. I'm *eighty-nine* years old, for pity's sake. Getting out of bed every morning represents a health and safety risk.'

'So how do you get your tea now?' I asked.

'They bring me three measly cups a day,' she said. 'One at nine o'clock, one at eleven and one at five. I look forward to them for hours before, but in the end, I'm always disappointed. They bring the tea upstairs on a trolley, and by the time it gets here, it's ice-cold, and strong enough to trot a mouse across. Bleurgh!'

She shook her head, and the loose skin on her face wobbled. I didn't know whether to laugh or cry.

Ella was trying very hard. 'So anyway, Gigi,' she said. 'What exciting things have happened around here since my last visit?'

Gigi took so long to answer, I thought maybe she'd fallen asleep. Then I looked at her face, and I could see that it was all crinkled up, like Ella had just asked her the hardest question in the world.

'Oh,' she said in the end. 'I've thought of something. We had ice-cream for dessert yesterday – strawberry flavour – my favourite.'

Strawberry ice-cream is OK, but how could it be the most exciting thing in your life?

I remembered when Gigi was the funniest person I knew.

At Halloween, she used to dress up as a witch, to scare all the trick-or treaters.

When she made popcorn, she never put a lid on the pan. She said it was much more fun to watch Ella and me racing madly around the kitchen, picking it up off the floor.

Just last year, she borrowed Ella's scooter, and scooted the whole way around the town, making rude gestures at anyone who pointed at her.

How could her life have changed so much, so quickly?

'Hey,' said Ella. 'I nearly forgot, I've got something to show you, Gigi. Uncle Greg sent me a video of Pedro playing in the garden in Tipperary.'

She held her phone out and we watched as Pedro galloped around on the grass, and rolled in a pile of leaves, barking like a crazy thing. When the video ended, no one said anything for ages.

Gigi spoke first. Her voice was all soft and whispery. 'I miss Pedro so much,' she said. 'I miss the way he got excited whenever I walked into the room. I miss the warm weight of him on my lap when I'm relaxing in the evening. I don't think I'll ever get used to not having that.' Ella stroked her arm, and Gigi continued, 'He looks happy,' she said.

I wondered if that made things better or worse. Did she mind that Pedro didn't seem to miss her?

'I'm glad he's happy,' she said then. 'I'm glad he's not pining for me. Thank you for showing me that, Ella, sweetheart. You're a kind girl.'

ᵕ̈ ☺ ☼

We only stayed for about half an hour, but it felt like a hundred years.

'Poor Gigi,' I said, as Ella used the code to let us out of the building. 'She was always so lively and funny and now she's so sad.'

'She tries her best to be positive,' said Ella, 'but she's not doing very well. Often when Mum and Dad and I visit, Gigi's eyes are all red. I think she cries a lot when we're not there.'

'That's awful,' I said.

'I know, but what can we do? We can't make time go backwards. We can't make Gigi young and strong again. The doctors say she'll never be able to go back to her own home.'

'Can we do *anything* to fix this?'

'Mum says we just have to be patient. She says all we can do is visit as often as we can, and hope that Gigi will settle in after a bit.'

'That's not good enough,' I said. 'We've *got* to help her. We've just got to.'

Ella smiled. 'Thanks, Eva,' she said. 'I knew I could rely on you.'

Chapter Three

Maths was the last class next day. I've always hated maths – mostly because it doesn't make a whole lot of sense to me. It's weird – the more I study it, the less I understand. It's like just thinking about maths eats up half of my brain.

Mrs Hegarty went straight up to the whiteboard and switched it on.

'Pay attention students,' she said. 'Today we're going to work on some problems.'

'Hard ones, I hope,' said Andy, who thinks he's the coolest kid in the class and likes to be best at *everything*.

He ran his fingers through his hair, making it all spiky, and one of the girls sitting near him looked like she was going to faint from excitement. Andy smirked and did it again.

'The questions we did last week were pathetically easy,' he said.

Mrs Hegarty ignored him. 'The first problem is very interesting,' she said.

'That would be a first,' I whispered.

Ella laughed, but stopped quickly when she saw that Mrs Hegarty was glaring at us. Our maths teacher is not known for her sense of humour.

I read the words on the screen:

Last month, Maria spent a fifth of her pocket money on books and ½ on phone credit, and she put the remaining 12 Euro into her bank account. Now answer the following questions:

For one second, while we waited for Mrs Hegarty to reveal the questions, I sat up and began to pay attention. Maybe this wasn't going to be as boring as usual. But then she showed the questions and I sat back again.

Does it matter what fraction of her money Maria saved?

Who cares what fraction of her money Maria spent in total?

If I were in charge, I could think of *way* more interesting questions.

Why did Maria spend so much on phone credit when she could be using WhatsApp and FaceTime?

Since she manages to save 12 Euro a month, did Maria's parents ever think that maybe they were giving her too much pocket money? (I haven't saved a single cent for years.)

Did Maria ever think about joining the library?

I hadn't even started the first part of the question when our scary principal, Mr Dean, marched into our classroom. I hadn't done anything wrong (as far as I knew), but still I felt guilty. Mr Dean has that effect on people.

Then I noticed that Mr Dean wasn't alone. 'Hurry along,' he said to someone who was still outside the classroom door. 'I haven't got all day. I've got a school to run.'

A girl walked into the classroom. She was tall and athletic looking, and her uniform was a bit too short and a bit too tight – like it belonged to someone else. As she walked, her braids rattled together, making small clinky, clattery sounds. I wondered if the noise kept her awake at night.

I felt sorry for this girl I'd never met. I knew exactly how she felt, because it wasn't so long since I'd had to start in a new school. When you're new in a place, the last thing you want is to be marched into the middle of a class and have a whole crowd of strangers staring at you, judging you.

'This is Aretta,' said Mr Dean. 'And she's come aaaaall the way from Nigeria.'

Behind Mr Dean's back, Aretta gave the tiniest roll of her eyes. I smiled to myself. This girl looked like she might be fun.

Mrs Hegarty went over to Aretta and shook her hand. 'You are very welcome to Ireland,' she said in a too-loud, too-slow voice. 'I hope you will be very happy here. When did you arrive?'

'Eight and a half years ago,' said Aretta, and everyone except for Mrs Hegarty and Mr Dean laughed.

When Mr Dean left, Mrs Hegarty found Aretta a place to sit at the front of the room, and then she started on another totally stupid and impossible question about children and sweets and x's and y's.

After what felt like a hundred years, Mrs Hegarty gave us a mountain of homework I was never, ever going to be able to do, and the class was finally over.

I packed up my books as quickly as I could. 'Come on,' I said to Ella. 'Hurry up. I can still remember what it's like to be the new kid. It's not nice being the only one on your own. Let's go over to Aretta, and ask if she'd like to hang out with us for a bit before going home.'

'That's really nice of you, Eva,' said Ella. 'Just give me a sec to get my stuff together.'

One minute later, we went over to where Aretta had been sitting, but there was no sign of her.

How had she managed to leave so quickly?

It was almost like she'd vanished into thin air.

'That's weird,' said Ella. 'She was here a second ago!'

'Maybe she was rushing off somewhere,' I said. 'Anyway, it looks like we'll have to wait until tomorrow to talk to her.'

'I guess,' said Ella. 'Do you still want to hang out?'

'Sure,' I said. 'Let's go to my place, and you can distract me from my maths homework.'

Chapter Four

Mum gave Ella and me a glass of home-made lemonade and we took them upstairs.

'Your room is so great,' said Ella, as she sat on my bed. 'It's like something out of a magazine. The rug your mum made for the floor is totally cool, and I love the way your dad painted those stripes on the wall.'

'Thanks,' I said, as I sat down next to her. 'But you never saw my bedroom in my old house, did you?'

She shook her head. 'I didn't know you back then, remember – and you never talk much about those days.'

'That's not an accident.' I said. 'My life was very different then, and I was a bit of a princess. I don't think you'd have liked me very much.'

'And you think I actually like you now?'

She ducked to avoid the cushion I threw at her, and then I continued.

'Anyway, back then I used to live in a house that was almost as big as a castle. My bedroom was *huge*, with its own bathroom and dressing room and heaps of cool stuff.'

'Wow!'

'I hated it here at first,' I said. 'I thought my life was over when Mum and Dad lost their jobs, and we had to move.'

Ella giggled. 'Was that when you went to see Madam Margarita, the fortune-teller, and you thought she could solve all your problems?'

I giggled too as I remembered. 'Yeah. Even though Madam Margarita turned out to be Ruby's mum who had no special powers at all.'

'I've never changed schools, and I've lived in the same house for my whole life. I guess all that moving around must have been hard for you,' said Ella, when we'd stopped laughing.

'It was – but that's only because I was totally spoiled. Back then I didn't know it was possible to live without fancy cars and exotic holidays.'

'Do you ever wish you could go back to your old life?'

'Sometimes – sort of. I wouldn't mind having a few more nice clothes, and I'd *love* a new smartphone. Mostly though, I'm happy now.'

'Good,' said Ella. 'And look on the bright side – if you hadn't moved here, you wouldn't have got to know me. Think what a disaster that would have been.'

'You're so weird,' I said, laughing.

'Speaking of weird,' said Ella, taking her phone out of her pocket. 'Have you heard this song? It's—'

'Shhh,' I said. 'Listen.'

'What? I don't hear anything.'

'There,' I said. 'There it is again.'

Ella rolled her eyes. 'Sounds like a dog barking – how totally amazing is that?'

'That dog belongs to Gemma, the woman next door,' I said, ignoring her sarcasm. 'And I've just had the most amazing idea ever.'

☽ ☺ ☼

'We'll be back in a bit, Mum,' I called as we went downstairs and outside.

Ella followed me without arguing. She trusts me, which can sometimes be a bit of a responsibility. She waited patiently on the footpath, while I ran into Gemma's house.

'What on earth *is* that?' she asked when I came back outside a minute later.

I giggled. 'It's a dog.'

'But it looks more like a horse.'

'It's a Great Dane,' I said. 'Her name is Jessie, and Gemma said I can borrow her for a bit. We can take her for a walk.'

Ella smiled. '*Now* I get it. You want to bring Jessie to visit Gigi?'

'Exactly,' I said, gripping the lead tightly and trying to stop Jessie from dragging me across the road.

'That's a really nice idea, but......'

'Don't worry – I know Jessie's a giant, but she's very gentle.'

'That's not what I'm worried about. Gigi loves all dogs, and they love her. I think she could tame a pack of wild wolves if she needed to.'

'So what's the problem?'

'Have you forgotten Nurse Witch – the wickedest nurse in the world? There's no *way* she's going to allow Jessie into the nursing home.'

I shrugged. 'We don't know until we try, do

we? Now let's go before Jessie pulls my arm off.'

‿ ☺ ☼

We hesitated on the driveway of the nursing home. Inside we could see Nurse Witch sitting at the reception desk, like a sentry at a watch-post. She looked like she was just waiting for something to go wrong. I wondered if she had a loaded gun hidden under the desk. Maybe she had a walkie-talkie in her pocket so she could call helicopters and jeeps and armed men with funny nets on their helmets.

'I'm not so sure about this,' said Ella. 'Nurse Witch is definitely going to say no when we ask if we can bring Jessie in.'

'Maybe she will, but do you have any other suggestions?'

'We could try smuggling her in?'

I giggled. 'Sure. That sounds like a great plan. You create a distraction, and then no one will *ever* notice me sneaking in with a Great Dane under my arm.'

Ella giggled too, but stopped suddenly. I looked up and saw Nurse Witch marching towards us. She flung the glass door open, and glared at us.

'What on *earth* do you think you're doing here with that ... with that beast?'

'Her name's Jessie,' I said, trying not to show how scared I was. 'I thought we could bring her in to see Gigi.'

'Gigi really, really misses her own dog,' said Ella.

'And there's a lot of research that says animals can be a calming influence on old people,' I added. 'Jessie's very sweet and gentle, and—'

As if she was trying to agree with me, Jessie lurched forwards and licked Nurse Witch's hand. Nurse Witch jumped backwards, shrieking.

'It's attacking me! It's attacking me! Get it away from me at once.'

'Sit, Jessie,' I said, and Jessie obeyed immediately, looking up at me with her huge brown eyes.

No one said anything while Nurse Witch ran inside and used about a litre of hand sanitizer to scrub her hands.

When she came back, her voice was hard and cold. 'Under *no* circumstances is that monster going anywhere near my residents. If the fright doesn't kill them all stone dead, they'll probably catch some deadly disease.'

'Jessie's had all her vaccinations,' I said. 'Her owner thinks ...'

I stopped suddenly when I saw that Nurse Witch looked really, really angry. I knew I was wasting my time. This woman was never, ever going to let Jessie inside. It was time to lower my expectations.

'Maybe I could bring Jessie around to the

back door,' I said. 'And Gigi could come outside to see her there?'

Now Nurse Witch's face went a scary purple-red colour, and I half-expected to see smoke coming out of her ears.

'I have never heard anything like this in my whole life,' she said. 'It is completely out of order. Get that beast off this property before I call the police.'

For a second I didn't move. She had to be bluffing, didn't she?

'You know you're ignoring years and years of research?' I said. 'Dogs can—'

Nurse Witch pulled her phone from her uniform pocket, and started to press numbers. I don't know if they actually send dogs or children to jail, but I wasn't hanging around to find out.

'You go on up to see Gigi,' I said to Ella. 'And tell her I said "hi". Come on, Jessie. We know where we're not wanted.'

'Thanks anyway, Eva,' said Ella, looking really sad and hopeless. 'It was nice of you to try to help.'

'Tell Gigi to look out her bedroom window,' I called, as Ella and Nurse Witch went inside. 'If that's not against the rules!'

Nurse Witch turned and glared at me. If this was a fairy-tale, I think I'd have turned to stone.

A few minutes later I was standing across the road, looking up at Gigi's window. Jessie was sitting on the footpath next to me, looking angelic. Upstairs, Gigi was leaning on Ella's arm and waving out at us. I picked up one of Jessie's huge paws and made her wave back. Gigi put her head down. It was hard to be sure from such a distance, but I think she might have been crying.

Chapter Five

'There's Aretta,' I said to Ella when we got into history class the next morning. 'Let's go sit near her.'

'Hey, Aretta,' I said as I sat down in the seat in front of her. 'We didn't get a chance to talk yesterday. I'm Eva and this is Ella.'

'Hi,' said Aretta.

For a second I was distracted by her perfect white teeth, and her beautiful smile. Too late, I realised I had no idea how to continue the conversation. There was a long, awkward silence

'Er, Aretta is a nice name,' I said in the end.

'Thanks,' said Aretta. 'It's Nigerian. It means charming.'

'Ella's real name is Petronella,' I said. 'And we don't even want to think about what that means.'

What I'd said wasn't very funny, but we all laughed – a forced laugh that went on for a few seconds too long.

'Er, do you miss Nigeria?' I asked. It was kind of a dumb question, but I was under pressure, and Ella was *no* help as she was pretending to be busy getting her history books in a perfect line.

Aretta acted like my question wasn't stupid at all.

'I miss Nigeria occasionally,' she said. 'But I left a long time ago, when I was very young. Sometimes it hardly feels real – like I only dreamed of my old life in Africa.'

'So have you really been in Ireland for eight and a half years, like you told the teacher?' I asked.

Aretta nodded.

'So where've you been all this time?' asked
Ella. 'How come we've never seen you before?
Did you go to a different school?'

'We used to live in Kilkenny. We only
moved here last week.'

I wanted to ask why she had moved, but
thought it might sound a bit rude. Now I
didn't know what to say. This was turning out
to be totally awkward. At the back of the class
there was a big crash as someone dropped a
book, and as Aretta turned her head, her braids
clinked together.

'I love your braids,' I said. 'They're really
cool – and it must be great not having to comb
your hair every morning.'

'Thanks,' she said. 'When I was little, my
mum always braided my hair for me, and now
I keep it like this, to remind me of her.'

Now I really, really didn't know what to say.

Why didn't Aretta's mum braid her hair anymore?

Why did Aretta need to be reminded of her?

I could feel my face going red. I desperately wanted to change the subject, but I couldn't figure out how to do it.

'She stayed in Nigeria,' said Aretta then. 'My mum, I mean. Her parents are very old, and she has to take care of them. So I came here with my dad and my brother.'

I tried to imagine a life where my dad would take me half-way across the world, leaving my mum behind – but I couldn't.

'Dad moved here for me,' said Aretta. 'For me and my brother. Because of my dad's political beliefs, we were always going to have problems in Nigeria.'

My face was still red, but I was relieved to see that Aretta didn't look like she was going to burst into tears.

'That's sad,' said Ella, suddenly looking up.

'You must miss your mum.'

'I do,' said Aretta. 'Every day. There's a computer where I live, and sometimes I Skype my mum. Sometimes, when she smiles at me, I can nearly forget that she's so far away. Sometimes I want to reach out and touch her, but of course that's impossible.'

'I'm so sorry,' I said, and then, even though it was probably a bit cowardly, I changed the subject.

'Does your brother go to this school too?' I asked.

Aretta shook her head. 'No. He's eighteen, and he finished school last year. He mostly lives in Dublin – he has a girlfriend there.'

I know Dublin isn't a million miles away, but it's not exactly next door either. It's not like Aretta could hang out with her brother any time she liked. It had to be rotten for her, being so far away from half of her family.

'Hey,' I said then. 'Ella and I are going into

town for a bit later. Do you want to come with us?'

'Thanks,' said Aretta. 'But I can't. I've got a piano lesson straight after school.'

'Oh,' I said, not sure why I felt so disappointed. 'Maybe we can do something tomorrow instead?'

Aretta smiled, but her smile wasn't as bright as before.

'Maybe,' she said, and before anyone could say anything else, the teacher walked into the classroom, and we had to endure an hour of totally boring discussion on the history of farm machinery – like anyone cared!

Chapter Six

The next day was Friday. Aretta wasn't in any of our morning classes, so Ella and I didn't see her until we were getting changed for PE after lunch.

'Hey,' I said, trying not to stare at Aretta's old and faded track-suit, and her runners that were starting to split down one side.

'Hey,' said Aretta. 'PE is my favourite subject. What do you think we'll be doing today?'

'Definitely badminton,' I said.

'How do you know?' asked Aretta. 'Is it always badminton on Fridays?'

Ella giggled. 'The teacher, Mr Holland, hates the rain, so if there's a cloud anywhere within a hundred miles, he won't bring us out to the playing pitches. That means we have to play badminton in the hall.'

'And do you like badminton?' asked Aretta.

'I guess it's OK,' I said.

'I *love* it,' she said. 'I used to play a lot when I lived in Kilkenny. Do we play in teams?'

'Here we play knock-out competitions,' I said. 'And there's this boy, Andy, who thinks he's the best badminton player in the world.'

'Andy probably *is* the best badminton player in the world,' sighed Ella. 'He wins the competition every single week. He played against the sixth-year boys one week, and he beat all of them too.'

'We don't mind Andy winning,' I added. 'The problem is that he goes on and on and on about it. He's a total pain. He's.......'

But Aretta wasn't listening any more. She'd

finished tying her laces and she was already on her way out of the changing rooms.

'That was a bit rude,' said Ella.

I smiled. 'Maybe,' I said. 'But something tells me this PE class is going to be *very* interesting.

⟨ ☺ ☀

'Oh, dear. Poor you.' said Ella when I told her that I was drawn to play Andy in the first round of the competition. 'But look on the bright side – at least you'll get a nice break while the rest of the competition is going on.'

I didn't answer. Losing a badminton match isn't the biggest tragedy in the world, but being first up against Andy and being totally humiliated in public – that's just rotten. I wondered if it was too late to pretend to be sick. Come to think of it, I did feel kind of sick at the thought of the match ahead.

'Hey, Mr Holland,' I said, trying to sound

weak. 'I think……'

But before I could finish, Andy was in front of me, strumming his badminton racquet like it was a guitar. He probably thought he was cool, but he really looked like an idiot

'Hey, Eva,' he said. 'I've never played you before. Are you sure you're ready for this?'

And suddenly, even though I knew it was pathetic, I really, *really* wanted to beat him. I jumped up from my bench. 'Sure I am,' I said. 'Bring it on.'

The first shuttle flew past my ear like a rocket. I didn't even see the second one, and the third one hit me on the head. The game was over in about a minute and a half – and I hadn't won a single point.

Andy jumped up and down, like he'd just beaten the Olympic champion.

'Yesss!' he said. 'Now who's next?'

Ella put her arm around me as I came off the court.

'Don't feel bad, Eva,' she said. 'Remember no one's ever got the better of that boy.'

Next to her, Aretta was smiling, and swinging her racquet to warm up. Suddenly I felt like I could read her mind.

'Don't even think about it,' I said. 'He's just too good.'

But Aretta kept on smiling. 'I'm not so bad myself,' she said.

☽ ☺ ☼

By the time the final between Andy and Aretta came around, the class was going crazy. We were all jumping up and down on the benches, screaming for the person we wanted to win. (That meant most of the class screaming for Aretta, and a few of the silly girls screaming for Andy because they like his hair and think he's cute.)

Andy and Aretta walked on to the court, and everyone clapped, like it was the final of Wimbledon or something.

'Quiet, please,' said Mr Holland, and amazingly, everyone obeyed. The sudden silence was weird, and a bit scary.

Andy was jogging on the spot like a mad thing. On her side of the court, Aretta stood up straight and tall. She looked calm and confident.

'OMG,' I whispered to Ella. 'Maybe she can do this.'

'Really?' asked Ella. 'You really think she can beat Andy? I know she's already won five matches … but Andy?'

I smiled and squeezed her hand. 'Let's just hope.'

I wasn't feeling so hopeful when Andy won the first ten points. In between jumping up and down, and doing stupid practice swings, he was grinning like his face was going to explode.

'Come on, Aretta!' I called. 'Don't let us down.'

And then it was like Aretta turned into a different person. She raced around the court, and no matter where Andy hit the shuttle, she was there, ready to hit it back. It was like she knew where he was going to hit it before he even swung his racquet.

Andy won a few more points, but basically the game was over. When Mr Holland called the final score 21-14 to Aretta, most of the class screamed and ran onto the court.

'You genius!' I shouted in Aretta's ear. 'You absolute genius! Why didn't you tell us you were so good?'

'I didn't know it was such a big deal,' she said, looking a bit embarrassed. 'Badminton is only my second favourite sport.'

'So what's—?' I began, but I couldn't finish as more people came over to hug Aretta.

I turned and saw Andy slipping away towards the boys' changing room.

'Do you feel sorry for him?' asked Ella.

'Nearly,' I said. 'But not quite.'

☺ ☺ ☼

When Aretta finally got into the changing room, she sat next to Ella and me.

'We're going to stop for hot chocolates before going home,' I said, when we were nearly dressed. 'There's a really cool place just down the road from here. The hot chocolate is totally yummy, and you can have all the marshmallows you like. Do you want to come with us?'

'I can't,' said Aretta. 'Thanks anyway.'

Suddenly I felt stupid. I looked at Aretta's shabby uniform and old-fashioned shoes and realized that she probably couldn't afford to pay for a hot chocolate.

'Our treat,' I said quickly.

'To welcome you to our school,' said Ella, smiling.

I hoped that smile meant she could pay for

half of Aretta's hot chocolate, as I knew for sure that I only had 2.50 in my pocket – and some of that was supposed to be for a new maths copy.

'That's very nice of you,' said Aretta. 'But I'm busy. I've got a ballet class in a few minutes. Thanks for asking though. See you on Monday.'

And then she grabbed her bag and was gone.

'Busy girl,' said Ella.

'Have you seen the way she's dressed?' I said. 'I'm not being mean or anything, but her uniform's ancient, and her schoolbag is falling apart. If she can't afford to get proper school stuff, where's she getting the money for piano and ballet lessons?'

'We've seen how good she is at badminton. Maybe she's amazingly talented at ballet and piano too, and she's getting some kind of scholarship for gifted kids?'

'Possibly, but I don't think that's it. Trust me, Ella, there's something weird going on with that girl, and I'm going to find out what it is.'

Chapter Seven

Most Friday nights I sleep over at Ella's place – it's a tradition we've had since we made friends. Her parents were just going out when I got there.

'Why does Alyson have to babysit?' Ella was saying. 'Why can't you trust me and Eva to stay here on our own? In some countries, I'd be working for a living by now – or I could be married.'

Ella's dad used to be my teacher, and it took me ages to get used to seeing her arguing with him. By now I'd had plenty of practice, though; Ella had the exact same argument with

her mum and dad every single Friday night. I
knew most of the lines off by heart.

'We know you're not a baby,' said her mum.

'And it would be nice if you *did* get a job,'
said her dad. 'We could do with a new car.'

'And I'd love one of those new high-tech
tennis racquets,' said her mum.

Ella rolled her eyes, 'I'm *serious*.'

Her mum hugged her. 'I know you are,
darling,' she said. 'And you're a good girl, but
you're still young. If we left you alone, and
something bad happened, we'd never forgive
ourselves. So the argument is over – again.
OK?'

Ella gave a big loud sigh, but she didn't argue
any more. Her parents are really nice, but once
they've made their minds up about something,
nothing will ever change it. I don't know why she
bothers with the Friday night row – habit I guess.

Her mum and dad hugged her, then waved
at me.

'Be good, girls,' her mum said. 'We'll be home at midnight.'

Then they left, closing the door behind them.

'Where's Alyson?' I asked.

'Where do you think? She's watching TV as usual. That girl is addicted.'

I went and stood at the door of the living room. 'Hey, Alyson,' I said. How's it going?'

'Hey,' she said without even looking up.

'We're going up to my room,' said Ella. 'Is that OK?'

'Sure,' said Alyson. Once again she didn't look up.

'Or we might go to a night club,' I said. 'And hang out with a few older boys for a bit.'

Ella giggled, but Alyson didn't react at all. 'Sure,' she said. 'Give me a shout if you need me.'

I wondered how much Ella's mum and dad were paying her to mind us. I hoped it wasn't very much, because Alyson was a waste of space as a babysitter. She just watched TV and ate crisps and let Ella and me do whatever we wanted. Luckily it didn't matter though – Ella and I are totally sensible.

Usually.

☺   ☺   ☼

'How's Gigi?' I asked when we got to Ella's room.

'Not so good,' said Ella. 'It was nice of you to bring Jessie to see her, but I think it only made her sadder than before. She kept saying what a beautiful dog Jessie was and how much she wanted to cuddle her. She said that hugging a dog makes you feel good in a way that nothing else can.'

'That's so sad.'

'I know. I can't stop thinking about her. I can't believe that wicked Nurse Witch sends her to her room at eight o'clock.'

'And what's she meant to do for the rest of the night? Is she allowed visitors?'

'Since Nurse Witch showed up, all visitors have to leave at 7.30 – and Gigi has nothing to do after that.'

'Does she like reading?'

'She used to love it, but now she finds it hard, because her eyes are so weak.'

'What about TV?'

'There's a TV in her room, but Gigi has always hated TV. She says she wants to live life, not watch other people pretending. She says there should be a law against reality TV.'

'So how does she pass the time?'

'She just goes to bed and lies there for hours.'

'She goes to bed before eight o'clock?'

Ella nodded. 'Yeah, there's nothing else for her to do – and it's really awful for poor Gigi. When she was at home, she always stayed up until one or two in the morning.'

'That's cruelty to old people if you ask me.'

'I agree. But what can we do?'

'We can definitely do something,' I said. 'I'm just not sure yet what it's going to be.'

☽ ☺ ☼

After that, we listened to music and chatted for a while. I couldn't enjoy myself though.

In the end I jumped up. 'I can't take this anymore,' I said. 'I can't stop thinking of Gigi lying alone in her room, staring at the ceiling. It's not like she's a prisoner. She hasn't done anything wrong.'

'I know,' said Ella, giggling. 'The only crimes Gigi's ever committed are crimes against fashion.'

'So let's go.'

'Where? What do you mean?'

'Let's go see Gigi. Let's see if we can cheer her up for an hour.'

Ella looked at her phone. 'But it's nearly ten o'clock.'

'Exactly. We'd better hurry up – we've only got two hours before your parents get back.'

'But…..'

'Come on,' I said. 'There's a few things I need to bring, so there's no time to waste.'

Chapter Eight

Alyson didn't even look up as Ella and I tip-toed past the living room. We let ourselves out the back door and circled around to the front of the house. A few minutes later we were standing behind a bush in front of the nursing home.

'Nurse Witch is there,' said Ella, looking through the glass at the woman sitting in the reception hall. 'Why does it have to be her every single day? Doesn't she *ever* go off duty?'

'Maybe she's not even human,' I said. 'Maybe she's a robot nurse.'

We giggled for a while, trying not to make any noise.

'So what are we going to do?' asked Ella.

'We're going to wait,' I said. 'Sooner or later, someone will ring their bell and Nurse Witch will have to go and see to them. Then we can let ourselves in, and go see Gigi.'

'Let's hope it's sooner rather than later,' said Ella. 'I'm freezing, and hanging around a car-park isn't exactly my idea of—'

Before she could finish, we saw a red light flash on the wall next to Nurse Witch's head. She made a grumpy face, and slowly got to her feet.

'Now's our chance,' I said. 'Be ready to run.'

Nurse Witch set off down the corridor, and Ella and I raced across the gravel. Ella keyed in the code and the door clicked open. We stepped inside and Ella headed for the lift.

'Stop,' I whispered. 'Nurse Witch will hear the ping as the lift opens, and she'll call the guards or shoot us or something. We've got to take the stairs.'

'But I don't know where ...'

She stopped talking and her face went pale. 'Nurse Witch is coming back,' she whispered. 'We're dead. We're totally dead.'

There was no time to escape by the front door. I grabbed Ella's hand and dragged her towards the only other door nearby. I pulled it open and saw that it was a cupboard full of walking sticks and walking frames. We threw ourselves inside and pulled the door almost-closed behind us.

I hardly dared to breathe as the squeak-squeak of Nurse Witch's shoes on the vinyl floor came closer and closer. I wondered what she'd do if she discovered us. Would we have to fight her off with the walking sticks?

Would we end up as headlines on the front page of the local newspaper? – *BIZARRE TWIST AS YOUNG GIRLS SNEAK INTO NURSING HOME!!*

But luckily, Nurse Witch hadn't noticed

anything strange. I peeped through a crack in the door and watched as she sat behind the desk, picked up the phone and pressed some numbers.

'Hi, Mammy,' we heard her say a second later. 'It's me. How are you? Yes, I'm fine, thanks…. Yes, I'm doing what you told me and eating lots of fruit and vegetables … Yes, I remember to wear my warm coat when I go out … Yes, Mammy, I'm getting enough sleep.'

In the cupboard, Ella and I tried to keep our giggling quiet.

'Mammy sounds like a total pain,' I whispered.

'Now we know where Nurse Witch got her bullying ways from,' Ella whispered back.

Nurse Witch's boring conversation went on for ages and ages. It was hot and uncomfortable in the tiny cupboard, and my head started to hurt.

After a bit, Ella edged a walking frame

towards the back of the cupboard and made a bit more room for us.

'Hey,' I said, as I peeped out through the crack in the door again. 'Don't get too settled. We're not staying long. Next time someone presses a bell, we're out of here.'

'But how are we going to find the stairs?'

'You know how people get obsessed with health and safety. I'm guessing there's a stairs at the end of each corridor, so whatever way Nurse Witch goes, we go the other way. Easy!'

I didn't feel as confident as I sounded, and when the red light flashed again, and Nurse Witch stood up, I noticed that my legs were a bit wobbly. Still though, we had to move – a whole night in a cupboard full of walking sticks wasn't exactly my idea of fun.

'Good-bye, Mammy,' said Nurse Witch. 'Yes, love you too. Talk tomorrow.'

'Get ready,' I whispered as she put down the phone. 'We're out of here.'

As soon as Nurse Witch's squeaky footsteps had faded away, I pushed the cupboard door open, and Ella and I raced in the opposite direction. We turned a corner, and I started to feel a small bit better when I saw a wide stairs at the very end of the corridor. Luckily, there was a thick carpet, and our feet made no sound as we scrambled up the stairs. When we got to the top, Ella recognised where we were, and led the way to Gigi's room. She pushed the door open and we slipped inside.

The room was in darkness, and as I closed the door I could just about see the shape of Gigi curled up in the bed.

'Nurse?' she said in a quiet voice. 'What's wrong? I didn't ring my bell.'

'It's not the nurse,' said Ella. 'It's me, Ella, and Eva's with me too. We've come to visit you.'

There was a fumbling sound, and then Gigi clicked a switch next to her bed. A pool of weak, yellowish light spread around us. Gigi looked at Ella and me for a long time.

'Am I dreaming?' she asked. 'If I am, it's the nicest dream I've ever had.'

'No, Gigi,' said Ella, leaning forward to hug her. 'It's not a dream. And anyway, you shouldn't even be asleep. It's not much after ten o'clock.'

'You're right,' said Gigi. 'I'm a grown woman, not a naughty child.'

She pulled herself up in the bed, threw off the covers and stood up. Her bony knees and long, knobbly toes were a bit sad, but I had to laugh when I saw that her nightie had a picture of a rock band, and a big slogan – *Here Comes Trouble!*

Gigi made her way across the room, and as she sat on her armchair, a huge smile spread slowly across her face.

'This is such a lovely surprise,' she said. 'And it's so kind of your mum and dad to let you out so late, Ella.'

Before Ella could answer, the smile faded from Gigi's face. 'What about Nurse Witch? Her rules are written in stone. How come she let you in here at this time?'

Ella looked at me, and I made a quick decision. Lies are usually wrong, and lies to an eighty-nine year old are probably worse than most.

'Actually, Nurse Witch doesn't know we're here,' I said. 'We sort of sneaked in.'

'*Sort of* sneaked in?' asked Gigi.

'We *actually* sneaked in,' said Ella, and she went on to describe our little adventure in the walking-stick cupboard.

Gigi laughed so much, I thought she was going to have a heart attack. 'You girls,' she said, wiping tears of laughter from her wrinkly cheeks. 'You're better than any medicine.'

'Does Nurse Witch ever come up stairs at night?' I asked.

'Sadly, yes,' said Gigi. 'And when she comes up, she pokes her ugly face into every single room to be sure that we're not getting up to mischief.'

'So she could come in here at any second?' said Ella, looking scared.

Gigi laughed. 'Not likely. Sometimes Nurse Witch's army training is a good thing. She comes up here to check on us at ten o'clock and at midnight. Otherwise, she stays downstairs unless someone on this floor rings their bell.'

'And how often does that happen?' asked Ella.

'Pretty much never,' said Gigi. 'Why would anyone want that wicked witch snooping around more often than necessary?'

'So we should be safe for a while,' I said. 'And that's lucky because we brought you something.'

I began to unpack my rucksack. Gigi

said nothing as I pulled out the kettle we'd borrowed from Ella's kitchen, three cups, tea-bags, a small jar of milk and a packet of chocolate biscuits.

'A midnight feast,' gasped Gigi. 'How wonderful! I feel like a girl again, having a midnight feast with my friends.'

It was a long way from midnight, and Gigi hasn't been a girl for nearly eighty years, but that didn't matter. I knew what she meant.

Chapter Nine

The kettle took ages to boil, and by the time it was ready, poor Gigi was practically jumping up and down on her chair. It was very sad to see how excited she was getting about a cup of tea.

'Hey, Eva,' said Ella. 'You make the tea. I've just thought of something, and I need to send a text.'

'OK,' I said, as I went to the corner and unplugged the kettle.

Ten minutes later, Ella and I were sitting on the bed, wrapped up in Gigi's soft crocheted blanket. We were sipping our tea and chatting.

Over in the armchair, Gigi was dunking her third biscuit into her tea, and looking like she was in heaven.

When our tea was finished, Ella picked up her phone.

'OMG,' she said. 'It's time.'

I had no idea what she was on about. 'Is this something to do with the text you sent?'

'Yes. I was texting my cousin, Lucy, in Tipperary, and I needed to give her some time to get sorted.'

'OMG,' I said, suddenly understanding. 'You're a genius.'

Gigi was looking puzzled, but when Ella passed over her phone, a huge smile spread over her face.

'It's called FaceTime,' explained Ella. 'And look, there's Lucy.'

I went and stood behind Gigi's chair, so I could see the screen. Lucy was sitting on her bed and waving. 'Hi, Gigi. Hi, Ella. Hi, Eva,' she said.

Gigi waved. 'Hi, darling,' she said very loudly, like her voice had to carry all the way to Tipperary. 'How are you?'

'Shhh,' said Ella. 'You don't want Nurse Witch hearing you, do you?'

Gigi shook her head. 'No way, Jose,' she said.

'Anyway,' said Ella. 'Lucy has a surprise for you. Show her, Lucy.'

Lucy moved her phone and there was a sudden silence as Gigi saw Pedro curled up in her arms.

'Pedro,' Gigi said in the end. 'Pedro.'

As she said his name the second time, Pedro's ears popped up, and he reached out for the phone with his paws.

'My baby,' said Gigi. 'How are you my little baby? Are you missing your mummy?'

Pedro put his head to one side and stared at the phone.

'Can he see me?' asked Gigi.

'Yes,' I said.

'Oh, my goodness,' said Gigi, and then she made a clicking noise with her tongue.

Now Pedro started to whimper, and put his head up to the phone. A second later, the picture went all pink and blurry.

'OMG,' squealed Ella. 'He's licking Lucy's phone. That's so gross.'

But Gigi didn't think it was gross at all. She stroked the screen of Ella's phone, and whispered to her pet for ages and ages.

Finally, Pedro settled back into Lucy's arms, and looked as happy as a dog can. Then he gave a small stretch, and closed his eyes.

Gigi sat back in her chair. 'Good-night, baby,' she said. 'It was so nice to talk to you.'

After we'd all said our goodbyes, Ella clicked off her phone and we went back to sit on Gigi's bed.

Gigi was wiping her eyes. 'Don't worry girls,' she said. 'These are happy tears. I'm a lucky lady to have such sweet people in my life.'

☽　☺　☼

After a bit, Ella helped her granny back into bed, and snuggled next to her while I packed up the tea things. When I was finished, I sat and watched them for a bit. Gigi had her arms around Ella. They both had their eyes closed, and Gigi had a small smile on her old, wrinkled lips. They looked very peaceful.

At twenty to twelve I touched Ella's shoulder. 'We've got to go,' I whispered. 'Your mum and dad will be home soon.'

As Ella climbed out of bed, Gigi opened her eyes and smiled. 'You'll never know how special tonight was to me,' she said.

'We enjoyed it too,' said Ella, as she gently tucked the blankets around her. 'And we can't say exactly when, but we'll definitely do this again.'

'Promise?' said Gigi.

'We promise,' said Ella and I together, and I realised that I was already looking forward to it.

☻　☻　☼

We had no trouble sneaking past Nurse Witch on the way out. I guess my mum is right – practice makes perfect.

Back at Ella's place, we let ourselves in the back door. Once again, Alyson didn't look up as we tip-toed past the living room, and went upstairs to Ella's room. We changed into our pyjamas, and lay on Ella's bed.

Ten minutes later, we heard Ella's parents coming in. Ella and I ran out to the landing and watched as they went in to the living room.

'Everything OK, Alyson?' asked Ella's dad. 'Did the little monsters behave themselves?'

Next to me, Ella rolled her eyes.

'And did you find the treats I left for you,

Alyson?' asked Ella's mum.

'Yeah,' said Alyson. 'They were great, thanks. Only thing is, I wanted to make myself some coffee, but I couldn't find the kettle. It wasn't in its usual place.'

Suddenly I remembered that the kettle and the cups and stuff were still in my rucksack, just inside the back door.

'OMG,' whispered Ella. 'How are we going to explain this? We're dead.'

'No, we're not,' I said. 'Just give me a minute.'

I legged it downstairs, got the kettle and flung it onto the kitchen counter, just as Ella's parents and Alyson walked in to the kitchen.

'Oh, hello, Eva,' said Ella's dad. 'We were just looking for ...'

'... the kettle,' said Alyson. 'But it's there. Who put it there? Did you have it, Eva?'

'I just came down for a glass of water,' I said, smiling sweetly, and hoping no one was going to notice that the flex of the kettle was hanging down over the kitchen cupboard and swaying slowly back and forth.

'But if you couldn't find the kettle, Alyson,' I said. 'Why didn't you come up and ask Ella and me? We'd have been happy to help you find it, wouldn't we, Ella?'

'Sure,' said Ella, who had just walked in. 'Night, Mum. Night, Dad. Eva and I are going to bed. Hanging around in my room doing nothing makes me soooo tired.'

Chapter Ten

On Monday, Ella and I sat with Aretta for maths and history classes. She laughed for ages when we told her about our late-night visit to Gigi.

'That's so cute,' she said. 'I wish I could have seen Gigi talking to Pedro on Skype. I know how special that can be.'

'So what did *you* do for the weekend?' I asked.

'Oh,' you know,' she said vaguely. 'Just stuff.'

Then she changed the subject and told us a funny story from when she was a little girl in Nigeria.

As soon as the last class was over, I jumped up from my seat.

'Quick, Ella,' I said. 'I'm not giving Aretta the chance to escape again.'

Ella jumped up too, and we followed Aretta out of the classroom, walking right behind her like not-very-good secret agents.

In the corridor, Aretta stopped and looked through the glass door of the gym. Ella and I stopped suddenly too, almost bumping in to her.

'What's going on in there?' asked Aretta when she saw us.

'After-school basketball club,' I said. 'It's on every Monday at this time.'

Aretta gazed in through the glass for ages. I wondered what could be so interesting about a few kids in shiny outfits running up and down, bouncing a big heavy ball in front of them – and then, at last, I thought I understood.

'Aretta?' I said.

She turned and looked surprised to see me, like she'd forgotten that Ella and I were there. 'Oh,' she said. 'Sorry. I got a bit carried away.'

'When you said that badminton is your second favourite sport ...' I began.

Aretta smiled. 'Yeah, basketball's my favourite. I've always loved it. I was on my school's team in Kilkenny. We won the county championship three years running.'

'Sounds good,' I said. 'I know everyone goes on about how taking part is the most important thing, but winning's kind of cool too. You must have hated leaving such a great team.'

Aretta's smile faded. 'Yeah. It was awful – but ... well ... we didn't have a choice. We had to leave Kilkenny.'

I wanted to ask why, but couldn't find the words.

'You should join the basketball club here,' said Ella. 'They're always looking for new members.'

'And if you're as good at basketball as you are at badminton, they'll love you,' I added.

Aretta shook her head, and I had to duck to stop her from taking my eye out with one of her hair braids.

'No. I ... can't,' she said.

'You don't even have to pay,' I said quickly.

'It's an official after-school activity, and the coach is a volunteer,' explained Ella.

This time Aretta hesitated for a second, 'No. It's not the money. It's just that ... I've got to…
… well … I'm busy this afternoon.'

She looked at the clock at the end of the corridor.

'Oh, no,' she said. 'Look how late it is. I've got to go. Bye, Eva. Bye, Ella. See you tomorrow.'

And before either of us could say anything, our new friend had pushed her way out the door and disappeared.

'Are you thinking what I'm thinking?' asked Ella.

'Depends what you're thinking,' I said. 'What I'm thinking is that it's weird how Aretta's always so busy.'

'Exactly. Even the president of America isn't as busy as Aretta claims to be.'

'So why does she keep running off like that?'

'Maybe she just doesn't want to be friends with us?'

'Even though we're the coolest, funnest girls in the whole school?' Ella giggled, and I continued, 'Seriously though. I wouldn't mind if Aretta was always unfriendly, but she's not. Most of the time, it's like she really wants to hang out with us, but when home-time comes, she changes completely.'

'Maybe an evil witch put a spell on her. Maybe she turns into a stick insect or a pot-bellied pig if she's not home by four thirty.'

I laughed. 'Whatever it is, it's a total mystery

– and mysteries need to be solved.'

☽ ☺ ☼

'Should we ask Aretta to hang out with us for a bit?' asked Ella, as we packed up our books at the end of school the next day.

I shook my head. 'No, I don't think so. I know she's just going to say she's really busy or some—'

Ella poked me in the ribs and I turned around to see Aretta walking towards us.

'Bye,' she said. 'Sorry I can't hang around, but I've got a ballet class. See you tomorrow.'

And then she rushed off.

'Do you believe her?' asked Ella.

'Not for a second. For one thing, her ballet class is supposed to be on Fridays. And for another, I called my friend Victoria last night. She goes to the only ballet school in town, and she's never heard of Aretta.'

'So she's definitely been lying to us.'

'Yes, now hurry up. I want to find out what's going on.'

Ella looked worried. 'What do you plan to do? It's not like we can corner her in the schoolyard and force her to tell us the truth. And anyway, what Aretta does after school is her business. Maybe we should just leave her alone.'

'If it turns out that she doesn't want to hang out with us after school, that's fine,' I said. 'But ...'

'But what?'

'But maybe there's something bigger going on. Something we should know about. Something we could help her with.'

'And how are we going to find that out?'

'Easy. We're going to follow her and see where she's going.'

'I'm not really sure—'

'*I'm* sure,' I said. 'And if we don't hurry, we won't be able to find her. Now are you coming or not?'

With a big sigh, Ella shoved her last book in to her bag. 'I'm coming, I guess,' she said.

☽   ☺   ☼

We hurried outside. There were crowds of people in the schoolyard, but it was easy to see our tall friend with her distinctive hairstyle.

We followed her out through the gates, and along the road. I felt a bit like a detective on a TV show, ready to duck into a doorway if Aretta happened to look back. After a bit though, I stopped worrying. Aretta was walking quickly, and didn't seem to be paying any attention to her surroundings.

'I'm really not sure about this,' said Ella, as we waited to cross the main street. 'It's kind of invading her privacy, isn't it?'

'Kind of,' I admitted. 'But it's all in a good cause, so I think that makes it OK.'

Aretta kept walking for ages, and Ella and I

followed at what we hoped was a safe distance. Soon we were far out of town, and walking along a narrow, twisty road I'd never been on before.

'This is the middle of nowhere,' said Ella. 'No wonder the poor girl doesn't want to hang out with us after school. She has to save her energy for the walk home.'

Aretta had turned a corner, and a few seconds later we followed her. In front of us was a huge, very neglected-looking, building. You could see that it had once been blue, but now the paint was dull and peeling away. A crooked sign blew in the wind, and I could just about make out the faded letters – *Grand Hotel.*

'That doesn't look very grand to me,' muttered Ella. 'It's a wreck. No wonder Aretta didn't want us to come here.'

We watched as Aretta walked up the weedy driveway and waved at the security guard, who was standing at the bottom of the front steps.

'This is all a bit weird,' I said. 'It's …'

But just then, as Aretta was half way up the steps, she stopped and turned around.

I looked frantically at Ella, but there was nowhere to hide.

'Act casual,' I said. 'Make it seem like we're just out for a nice walk.'

But it was too late. Aretta was staring at us, and she didn't look happy. She looked like she hated us. She stamped up the last few steps and went in the front door, slamming it hard behind her.

'I don't understand,' said Ella. 'What *is* this place? It's like a prison or something. Why is there a security guard? Why is Aretta living here?'

And then I remembered.

'I've heard Dad talking about this place,' I said. 'He did some repairs on the roof last year.'

'And what did he say?'

'I can't remember all the details, but one

thing I do remember is that he said he wouldn't like to live here.'

'Poor Aretta.'

'You said it,' I repeated. 'Poor Aretta.'

☽ ☺ ☼

'Remember the old hotel you worked in last year?' I asked Dad at tea-time that night.

'Remember?' he said. 'I'll never forget it.'

'So what exactly is it?'

'It's called a direct provision centre. It's where asylum seekers have to live while the government decides if they can stay in Ireland or not.'

'And why do they come here in the first place?'

'All kinds of reasons,' said Mum. 'Sometimes people come because their race or religion isn't popular in their own country. Sometimes people seek asylum because they've disagreed with their government and are afraid of being punished.'

'So these people are lucky to be here, where they can believe or say whatever they want, and not get into trouble?' I said.

Dad made a face. 'That's the theory, but in my opinion, we don't treat these people very well. We feed them, and give them a roof over their heads, but we could do a whole lot more.'

'Anyway,' said Mum. 'Why the sudden interest in asylum seekers?'

'There's a new girl in our class, Aretta, and Ella and I think she might live in the old Grand Hotel.'

'You're not sure?'

'She never said. I don't think she wants to talk about it.'

'I wouldn't blame her,' said Dad. 'If I lived there, I wouldn't want to talk about it either. But if you want to invite Aretta over here some afternoon, she'd be very welcome.'

'That's a lovely idea,' said Mum. 'Why don't you invite her over for tea tomorrow?'

Chapter Eleven

I was just at the gate of the school the next day, when Aretta marched up to me. Her face was all tight and scary looking, and her eyes were huge and dark. I figured she probably wouldn't be coming for tea in my house any time soon.

I looked over my shoulder, hoping that Ella might be around, but there was no sign of her.

'Er ... hi, Aretta,' I said.

'You followed me!' she said. 'You and Ella followed me home. How *dare* you do that? Haven't you heard of respecting people's privacy?'

I thought about denying it, but decided that wasn't going to help. There was no way Aretta was going to believe me, and it would be just one more lie.

'I'm sorry,' I said. 'We *did* follow you. But we meant well, honest. You're always so nice during school time, but at the end of the day, it's like you turn into a different person. You rush off like there's a pack of wild dogs chasing you.'

'So going home straight after school is now a crime in this country?'

'Of course it isn't. But Ella and I were worried about you.'

'You don't have to worry about me. I'm perfectly fine.'

I took a deep breath. 'I know about the direct provision centre,' I said. 'My dad explained it all to me. I understand—'

'You understand *nothing*!' she snapped. 'You're just a spoilt, rich girl.'

'That's not fair. Both my parents lost their jobs, and ...'

But then I stopped. I thought of the lovely warm and cosy home I shared with my mum and dad. I thought of the ugly building where Aretta lived, far away from her mother and brother. Maybe Aretta was right. Maybe compared to her, I *was* spoilt and rich.

While I was still figuring out how to explain myself, Aretta marched off.

☽　☺　☼

'I met Aretta,' I said to Ella when I met her at break time.

'And?'

'You were right, Ella. I should have listened to you. Following Aretta home was a really bad idea. Now she's mad at us.'

'Maybe I should find her and say sorry?'

'I tried that, but I don't think she's ready to listen to our apologies. Like I said, she's totally mad. I can't really blame her, and I can't think of a way to change it.'

☺ ☺ ☼

Ella and I didn't see much of Aretta over the next few days. I'm not sure if she was avoiding us, or we were avoiding her. Maybe it was a bit of both.

By Friday I couldn't take any more. Even watching Aretta beating Andy at badminton didn't make me feel any better. After the match, I tried to congratulate her, but when she saw me coming she turned and walked away.

'This is awful,' I said to Ella as we walked home from school. 'We *have* to make Aretta understand how sorry we are.'

'Maybe we should buy her a present to say sorry?'

'That's a great idea,' I said. 'But what will we get her?'

Ella smiled. 'Just follow me,' she said. 'I know exactly what we should get.'

☺ ☺ ☼

'We're going to Maggie's house!' I said a few minutes later, as I followed Ella around the last bend.

'That's great. I haven't seen her for ages.'

Maggie is my friend, Ruby's, mum. Ruby used to go to our school, but she's an amazing swimmer, and now she goes to a special boarding school in London where they have swimming coaching every day.

'Have you heard from Ruby lately?' asked Ella, as she rang the front doorbell.

'Yeah. She messaged me last week. It was nice to hear from her, but ...'

'But what?'

'I miss her. I'm happy that she got that great swimming scholarship, but I wish it could have been in a school a bit closer to here.'

'So when did you last see her?'

'It was ages and ages ago. We message all the time, and I see pictures of her, but it's not the same. I'd love to just hang out with her for a bit, and ... you know ... talk properly. I'd love to ...'

I stopped talking as I heard Maggie's dog, Lucky, yapping madly. A second later, we heard the squeaking of Maggie's wheelchair as she approached the door.

'Eva! Ella!' said Maggie when she saw us. 'What a nice surprise. Come in. Sit, Lucky, and try and be good for once.'

I picked Lucky up and cuddled her. As she snuggled up against me, and licked my face, I had an idea.

'Maybe Ella and I could take Lucky for a walk sometime, Maggie?' I said.

'Of course!' said Maggie. 'Lucky loves walks and I don't have time to bring her as often as I'd like.'

By now we were inside Maggie's living room. She brought us lemonade, and then she told us all about Ruby's latest swimming championship. (I was too polite to tell her that Ruby had already sent me a hundred snapchats from it.)

'Anyway,' I said after a bit. 'As well as coming to see you, there's something we want. We'd like to buy one of the lovely bracelets you make.'

'Of course,' said Maggie. 'Is it someone's birthday?'

'Not exactly,' I said.

While Maggie took out a box of her amazing jewellery, I told her all about Aretta, and how we'd offended her.

'The poor girl,' she said. 'It can't be easy living in a place like that. And poor you, too, Eva. You're so kind-hearted, and I know you were only trying to help.'

I picked up a gorgeous green and mauve

bracelet. 'What do you think, Ella?' I asked. 'Will we get her this one?'

'Definitely. That's so beautiful, Maggie. You're a genius.'

Maggie put the bracelet into a small paper bag, and handed it to me. Ella and I started to count out our money, but Maggie shook her head. 'I won't let you pay for this one,' she said. 'It's a present for you to give to your new friend.'

'But that's not fair—' I began to protest.

Maggie laughed. 'Maybe you can do something for me in return.'

'Like what?' I asked.

Maggie moved her wheelchair slightly forwards, and I knew what she meant.

'Where's the oil?' I asked. 'Is it back in the shed again?'

'Yes,' sighed Maggie. 'I started to keep it near me, but I think Ruby tidied it up the last time she was home.'

Ella gave me a funny look. I guessed she was wondering how I knew where Maggie kept her oil.

'The first time Maggie and I met,' I said. 'I ended up oiling her wheels.'

'It was the start of a wonderful relationship,' said Maggie smiling.

I got up and headed for the back door.

'Be careful,' called Maggie after me. 'You might get lost and never be seen again. It's a jungle out there.'

'You weren't kidding,' I said, when I came back with the oil and began to squeeze a few drops onto Maggie's wheels. 'What happened to your garden? I half-expected to see a few tigers lurking in the shadows.'

Maggie sighed. 'Ruby used to keep it a bit tidy, but now that she's gone, it's completely neglected. I can't do anything about it because the paths are too narrow for my chair. I haven't been to the end of the garden since I had my accident.'

'My dad could probably fix that for you,' I said.

'That's kind of you to offer, Eva,' said Maggie. 'But it wouldn't be worth it. Even if the paths were made wider, the flower-beds are all too low for me to reach. Gardening is beyond me these days. Don't worry about it, though. I've learned to live with my limitations.'

'Oh, OK,' I said. I couldn't imagine what it would be like to be Maggie.

Maggie smiled at me, like she could read my mind. 'It's not as bad as you think,' she said. 'Now who's for more lemonade?'

Chapter Twelve

After tea that evening, I went over to Ella's place as usual. As soon as Ella had finished her weekly row with her parents, we went upstairs, and waited for them to leave.

'Let's go see Gigi,' said Ella when they were safely out of the way.

I laughed. 'You're very brave this week.'

'Actually I'm not. I'm still scared, but I'm hiding it better, that's all. Last week was fun, though, and Gigi absolutely loved it. It was all she could talk about when I visited her yesterday. She pretty much made me promise to come again tonight.'

'Do you think we should bring the kettle?' she asked, as I followed her downstairs.

'Of course we should. You know how Gigi loves her cup of tea.'

'But what if Alyson wants to make herself some coffee? We'll never get away with what we did last week – even Alyson's not ditzy enough to fall for the same thing twice.'

'Leave it to me,' I said. 'I've got a plan.'

I flicked on the kettle, and a few minutes later, I carried a cup of coffee into the living room. Ella walked behind me with a tray of biscuits and snacks.

'We brought you coffee and treats,' I said, and Alyson was so surprised, she actually paused the television and looked up.

'That's very kind of you,' she said.

'Oh, you're such a good baby-sitter,' I said. 'So we thought we'd do something nice for you. My mum always says a good deed is ...'

Ella nudged me and I realised I was getting a

bit carried away. I stopped talking and Ella and I backed out of the room.

'Anyway, Alyson,' said Ella. 'We'll be upstairs if you need us.'

'Sure,' said Alyson. But she'd already restarted the TV, and was lost in a whole other world.

'How are we going to explain?' asked Ella, as we waited for Maggie to answer the door.

'Leave it to me. And don't worry, Maggie's cool. She probably won't ask any awkward questions.'

'Back again, girls,' said Maggie, when she opened the door. 'Are you here to buy another bracelet?'

'No,' I said. 'This time we came to borrow Lucky. Remember we promised to bring her for a walk.'

When we said her name, and the word

'walk,' Lucky started to run around in circles, yapping with excitement.

'Isn't it a bit late for walking?' said Maggie. 'Maybe you should wait until tomorrow?'

Ella stared at me. So much for Maggie not asking awkward questions. I thought about lying, but decided against it. Even though she's not a fortune teller, Maggie's always been very good at seeing right through me.

'Actually, it's not just any old walk,' I said. 'We want to bring Lucky to see Ella's granny, who lives in a nursing home. She had to give her dog away, and she really, really misses him.'

'Oh, how sad! Bringing Lucky to see her sounds like a very nice thing to do,' said Maggie. 'After Ruby moved to London this house seemed very empty, and it didn't feel right until I got Lucky. She's been great company for me. And isn't your Granny lucky that pets are allowed to visit, Ella? Not all nursing homes are so open-minded.'

Ella and I didn't answer, and Maggie narrowed her eyes.

'You have checked to see that dogs are allowed, haven't you?'

'Oh, we've checked,' said Ella, telling the truth. 'You can trust us, Maggie, we're very familiar with the nursing-home rules.'

I tried not to smile. What would Maggie say if she knew that pets were totally banned from the nursing home and even humans weren't allowed there after seven-thirty?

'Well, that's fine, then. Just let me get Lucky's lead.'

When she came back with the lead, she looked worried again. 'Won't it be very late by the time you're finished visiting? Will one of your parents be able to pick you up?'

I smiled my best smile, and hoped that Maggie wouldn't notice how careful I was being with my words.

'Oh, Ella's Mum and Dad will be out

anyway – and they never mind picking us up if it's late.'

'OK,' said Maggie, clipping Lucky's lead on to her collar. 'Have a nice time. I go to bed early, so if there's no light on in the hall, you can just let Lucky in through the cat-flap on the side door.'

When she said the word 'cat-flap' she lowered her voice, as if Lucky might understand, and be insulted.

'Thanks, Maggie,' I said. 'We'll do that. Bye.'

'OMG,' said Ella, as we walked away with Lucky. 'We haven't even got to the nursing home yet, and already I'm exhausted. I think it's going to be a long night.'

☽ ☺ ☼

When we got to the gate of the nursing home, I took off my fleece, and wrapped Lucky up in it.

'No point taking chances,' I said. 'If Nurse Witch catches us on our own, she'll go crazy.

If she catches us with a dog, she'll go totally, totally crazy.'

Lucky didn't seem to mind being wrapped up, and she snuggled up against me, like she was getting ready for a snooze.

'Good doggie,' I whispered as we tiptoed towards the door. 'Just stay like that, and soon we'll be safely inside.'

Once again, Nurse Witch was on duty, and this time we didn't have to wait long before she was called away. Ella and I ran as quietly as we could across the gravel and let ourselves in.

We made it upstairs without any problem, and walked along the corridor towards Gigi's room.

'This is easy-peasy,' said Ella, as she opened the bedroom door. 'We could come here any time. We could—'

She stopped talking and looked really scared. I followed her into the room to see what was wrong. Gigi was dressed and sitting up in her armchair, but she wasn't alone. In the other chair was a tiny woman, all dressed up in a lacy cardigan and shawl.

'Oh, goodie,' said the woman. 'The party is starting at last!'

Chapter Thirteen

I pushed the door closed, and Ella and I stood in front of it, like we'd been turned to stone.

'I'm so glad you're here, girls,' said Gigi. 'We've been waiting and waiting. And we're dying for our tea, aren't we, Nancy?'

'Yes, indeed,' said Nancy. 'But sit down and have a little rest first. You must be tired after your journey.'

This was so weird. Without saying a word, Ella and I went to sit on the bed. I lay Lucky in a corner, still covered with my fleece.

The two old ladies looked sweet, as they smiled happily at us, like little kiddies waiting for a treat. I didn't know what to say.

Who was Nancy and why was Gigi acting like they were best friends?

I thought all the other residents of the nursing home were supposed to be boring old farts.

'Nancy isn't a boring old fart,' said Gigi, like she could read my mind. 'I thought she was, but I was wrong. So I invited her to join us for tea.'

'That was nice of you, Gigi,' I said weakly.

Nancy smiled a sweet smile. 'She didn't have a choice anyway. I heard you three talking last week, and threatened to tell Nurse Witch if Gigi didn't invite me to join you tonight.'

She had cute twinkly eyes, and I had no idea if she was serious or not. Was this a sweet old lady, or a big bully? I decided to keep Lucky hidden until I was sure. Fortunately, she seemed to have fallen asleep under my fleece.

'I'll put the kettle on,' said Ella. 'Does

everyone want tea?'

'Did someone say tea?'

The door was pushed open and an old man came in, leaning on a walking aid and shuffling slowly forwards in his slippers.

'I've brought cupcakes,' he said, nodding towards a big bag that was hanging from the walking aid. 'But my daughter-in-law made them, so they might well be poisonous – ha, ha!'

His laugh was loud and it really scared me. What if all this activity brought Nurse Witch upstairs? I *so* didn't want that! I looked at Gigi, but she didn't seem a bit worried.

'Oh, Fred,' she said. 'So glad you could make it. Will one of you girls get him a chair from the hall?'

I couldn't move without disturbing Lucky, so Ella went and got a chair and Fred lowered himself slowly into it.

'Is that everyone?' I asked, half-afraid of the answer.

'Oh, yes,' said Gigi. 'Now hurry up, Ella, and pour out that tea before we all die of thirst. If there aren't enough cups, you can use the glasses that are on the sink in my bathroom.'

A few minutes later, we were all settled with our tea and cakes. Despite what Fred had said, the cupcakes were delicious, and everyone had two. I crossed my fingers and hoped none of the old people was diabetic – I didn't want to be responsible for a health crisis in the nursing home.

The old people chatted and told funny stories about long-ago. Far from being boring old farts, it sounded like Fred and Nancy had lived very exciting lives. Fred was a sailor and had travelled all over the world. Nancy had been a great tennis player, and had won heaps of international tournaments. I felt sorry for them, living under such strict rules now.

After a bit, the tea and cakes were gone, and

the old people looked a bit sleepy.

Ella looked at me and nodded.

'Er, there's one other thing,' I said. 'We brought a surprise.'

All the grey heads popped up again. 'I *love* surprises,' said Fred. 'Is it a rude picture?'

'No,' I said, trying not to laugh. 'It's not a rude picture. It's this.'

As I spoke, I lifted Lucky up so they could see her.

Gigi looked like she was going to faint. 'A dog,' she whispered. 'You've brought us a dog. That's the sweetest, sweetest thing.'

She held her hands out, and I brought Lucky over to her. She was still sleepy, and she snuggled into Gigi's arms like a baby. Gigi stroked and kissed her and talked to her. 'My pet. My lamb. My little love. Who's the best, cuddliest doggie in the whole world? It's you, isn't it?'

This went on for ages and ages. It was like

Gigi had been saving up all the little things
she used to whisper to Pedro, and was letting
them out now. Lucky wagged her tiny tail,
and licked Gigi's fingers, and when Gigi's tears
of happiness fell on her coat, she didn't even
blink.

After a while, Fred and Nancy demanded
a turn at holding Lucky, and she was passed
around, like it was a game of pass the parcel.
She didn't mind, and went happily into each
pair of quivery, wrinkled old hands, like it was
the best thing ever.

'OMG!' said Ella in the end. 'Look at the
time. We've got to go.'

I jumped up and started to pack up the cups
and stuff. Ella went over to Nancy and held
her hands out.

'Sorry,' she said. 'But we've got to take Lucky
now.'

'Take her?' said Nancy.

'Isn't she staying here with us?' asked Fred.

'But pets aren't allowed,' I said. 'Nurse Witch would never let her stay.'

'Who said anything about Nurse Witch?' said Nancy. 'Lucky's only a little scrap of a thing. We can easily hide her here.'

'Once my friend smuggled a snake onto our ship,' said Fred. 'We kept him for months – until we got tired of catching mice for it to eat. Then we had to smuggle him back to the jungle – not easy, I can tell you.'

I looked desperately at Gigi. Surely she didn't think that we could just go off and leave Lucky there? Had we accidentally broken her heart again?

But she was walking over to Nancy, and she very gently took Lucky out of her arms.

'Say goodbye,' she said. 'Lucky has to go now. Her owner will be waiting for her.'

Nancy looked like she was going to cry.

'We'll bring her back next week,' I said. 'We promise.'

'Cross your heart and hope to die?' said Nancy.

'Er, we just promise,' said Ella.

I had finished tidying up, and Ella took Lucky from Gigi.

Gigi gave the dog a last kiss, and stood up as straight as she could. 'Well, I don't know about the rest of you,' she said. 'But it's past my bedtime.'

Nancy and Fred took the not very subtle hint. They hauled themselves to their feet and after Fred released the brakes on his walking aid, they began to shuffle towards the door.

I wondered if we could just go away and leave them to look after themselves.

What if Nancy needed help to get undressed?

What if Fred needed to use the toilet and couldn't manage on his own?

Were we going to have to do gross stuff?

'Er ... do either of you need any help?' asked Ella, obviously thinking the same.

'With anything?' I added.

'We are not babies,' said Nancy. 'We can manage perfectly well. But thank you for your kind offer.'

Gigi smiled at us. 'Despite the way Nurse Witch treats us, we can all look after ourselves just fine. One day that might change, but for now, we simply want to do what we can.'

We watched as Nancy and Fred slowly made their way to their rooms, and then Ella tucked Gigi into bed, pulling the covers up over her skinny body.

'Sleep tight,' she said. 'Don't let the bed-bugs bite.'

'You remember!' said Gigi.

'Of course I remember,' said Ella. 'You always used to say that to me when I was a little girl.'

She kissed Gigi on the forehead, and then we switched out the light and tip-toed from the room.

After that, everything went like a dream. We had no trouble sneaking past Nurse Witch. When we got to Maggie's place, I was glad to see that there were no lights on downstairs. We went around to the side of the house, and pushed the cat-flap open for Lucky.

'You should be proud of yourself,' I whispered. 'You were a big success and you made all those people very happy.'

Lucky wriggled around and licked my face, almost like she understood, and then she went inside.

When we got back to Ella's place, it looked like Alyson hadn't moved from the couch. We quickly replaced the kettle and cups, and went upstairs to lie on Ella's bed.

'That was a totally cool evening,' I said. 'Who knew that hanging around a nursing home could be such fun?'

'Yeah, it was great, wasn't it?'

'So you're on for next Friday?'

'Definitely. I think it's going to be the highlight of my week.'

Chapter Fourteen

'What's wrong with you today, Eva?' asked Mum on Monday morning. 'You're very quiet and you've barely touched your breakfast.'

'I know it's kind of stupid,' I said. 'But I'm really nervous about meeting Aretta.'

'That's not stupid,' said Mum. 'It's always difficult when a friend gets angry with you.'

'It's not so much the fact that she's angry,' I said. 'It's the fact that she's right. We never should have followed her. It was a rotten thing to do.'

'But you and Ella thought you were doing

the right thing.'

'Ella didn't even want to do it,' I said. 'It was all my idea.'

Mum smiled. 'Poor Ella. I know how persuasive you can be. Anyway, it's done now. All you can do is apologise again, give her that lovely bracelet, and hope that Aretta has calmed down over the weekend.'

'I guess,' I said. 'And just in case she hasn't, I've asked Ella to call for me here this morning. If Aretta's mad, I don't think I could face her on my own.'

Mum hugged me. 'You'll be fine,' she said. 'Now eat up, or you'll be late.'

☽ ☺ ☼

Ella and I got to school early, and hung around the playground. Everyone was pushing and shouting, but Ella and I didn't talk. I knew she was nervous too. Before too long, we saw Aretta arriving. I was kind of glad – when you're

dreading something, sometimes it's easier to grit
your teeth and get it over with.

It was easy to see Aretta making her way
across the playground. She was taller than
most of the girls and even some of the boys.
She was walking in a straight line, but when
she suddenly swerved to the left, I knew she'd
seen Ella and me.

'Come on,' I said to Ella. 'Let's get this over
with. We'll say what we have to say, and give
her the present. If she's still mad at us after
that, well there's nothing else we can do.'

'OK,' said Ella. 'Let's do it. I'm right behind
you.'

We pushed quickly through the crowd.
Aretta started to walk faster, and I guessed she
knew we were following her. I called her name
once, but she didn't look back. She was inside
by the time I was close enough to grab her
arm.

'Wait up, Aretta,' I said. 'We just want to

talk to you.'

Aretta stopped walking and turned towards us. She still looked angry. Beside me, I sensed Ella taking a step backwards.

'Please let me go,' said Aretta. 'I haven't got anything to say to you.'

'Won't you listen to us for one minute?' I said.

'Give us a chance,' added Ella.

For a second Aretta didn't reply. Then her face relaxed a tiny, tiny bit.

'This isn't a good time. I've got a class to go to.'

I realised she was right. This wasn't the kind of conversation you could rush through in two minutes, with kids shouting and pushing past you.

'We could meet after school,' I suggested. 'There's a park near here. It's on your way home.'

Ella nudged me, and I realised I shouldn't be

reminding Aretta that we knew how she went home.

'The park is just down the road,' Ella said. 'You can't miss it.'

'I can't hang around after school,' said Aretta. 'I've got ……stuff to do.'

'Fifteen minutes,' I said. 'Can you give us fifteen minutes?'

'Ten minutes,' said Aretta, as she turned to walk away. 'I'll see you there straight after school.'

'At least she didn't say no,' said Ella, as we walked to our French class.

'I guess,' I said. 'Now we've just got a few hours to plan the perfect speech.'

☽ ☺ ☼

The day dragged slowly on. I passed Aretta in the corridor a few times. She didn't smile, but she didn't look away either – I figured that was progress. In any classes we shared, she arrived late, and sat as far away from me as possible, without actually sitting in the corridor.

‿   ☺   ☼

Two minutes after school ended, Ella and I were sitting on a bench near the entrance to the park. It was a lovely day. Small kids were running around chasing pigeons. I felt a bit jealous of them. They could rely on their mums and dads to fix stuff for them. Ella and were older, and sometimes we had to fix our stuff on our own.

'Hey,' said Aretta, making me jump.

It was like she'd sneaked up on us. Maybe she was teaching us a lesson.

I slid across the bench to make room, but Aretta didn't sit down. She stood in front of us and folded her arms. I realised she hadn't been kidding when she said she was only going to listen to us for ten minutes.

'We're really, really sorry for following you

the other day,' said Ella.

'We can't even make any excuses,' I said. 'We meant well, but it was a dumb thing to do.'

Aretta didn't argue.

'We got you something,' said Ella. 'Just to show you how sorry we are.'

I held the paper bag towards Aretta. She kept her hands in her pockets and looked at it like she wasn't sure if it we were playing some kind of mean trick on her.

No one said anything for a while. Our time was running out, and I didn't want to spend our last minutes sitting there like statues. I took the bracelet out of the bag, and held it on the palm of my hand. For a second, I remembered the way I used to hold treats towards a timid pony, back in the days when I used to go horse-riding. The bracelet shimmered in the sunshine, and looked like an enchanted treasure from a kid's fairy-tale. Luckily the magic worked on Aretta.

'That's gorgeous,' she said, as she reached out and picked it up.

'Our friend's mum made it,' said Ella. 'She sells them in the market.'

Aretta put the bracelet on. It looked amazing against her dark skin.

'I love it,' she said. 'Thank you.'

'So we're forgiven?' I asked.

Aretta smiled for the first time since she'd arrived. 'I guess,' she said.

☽ ☺ ☼

After that it was easier. Aretta sat down beside us, and Ella told her about Ruby and her swimming scholarship, and how I had helped her, when she panicked on the day of the trials.

Then I told Aretta about the first time I met Ruby's mum, when she was pretending to be a fortune-teller. Aretta laughed a lot, but then she jumped up suddenly, almost like an invisible timer had beeped in her brain.

'I've got to go,' she said.

Ella and I stood up too. 'Oh,' I said. 'I nearly forgot. My mum and dad said you can come over to our place after school someday. Ella can come too, and we can hang out and do stuff.'

'I can't,' said Aretta.

I remembered the security guard outside her home. 'It's OK, I said. 'I understand if you can't invite me back to your place. That doesn't matter. You can still come to my place any time you want.'

'Or to mine,' said Ella. 'My parents love when I have friends over. They won't mind that we never go to yours.'

'It's not that,' said Aretta.

'Then what ...?'

I stopped myself. I didn't want Aretta to think I was all nosy and interfering again.

Too late.

'I'm busy after school every day,' said Aretta, with a strange, cold look on her face. 'And I don't have to explain why. Some things are private.'

'Sure,' I said. 'I understand.'

I didn't really understand, but there was nothing I could do about it.

'If you ever want to talk,' said Ella. 'Eva and I are good listeners.'

'Thanks,' said Aretta. 'But I'm fine. Now I really have to go. Thanks for the bracelet. See you at school tomorrow.'

☽ ☺ ☼

'I think that went OK,' said Ella when Aretta had gone.

'Yeah,' I said. 'It *was* OK. But I'd still love to know what that girl does after school. If she was really going to ballet or piano lessons, she would have said. She didn't mention activities though. She just acted all weird when I asked why she couldn't hang out with us – so there has to be something else. There has to be a reason she does her vanishing act every day at four o'clock.'

'Eva!' said Ella. 'Didn't you hear the girl? She doesn't want us to poke our noses into her life. She doesn't need our help.'

'*Everyone* needs help sometimes.'

'When she wants our help, I'm sure she'll ask for it, and until then, we'll have to back off.'

'But what if—?

'I'm not kidding, Eva. I know you're only trying to help Aretta, but there's nothing we can do. If we interfere in her life any more, Aretta's *so* not going to be happy.'

'But—'

'*Forget* it, Eva. If we make Aretta mad again, all the bracelets in the world won't be able to fix it.'

I didn't like what she was saying, but I knew she was right.

'I guess,' I said. 'Now do you want to come to my place and help me with my maths homework? I have *no* idea how to do it.'

☽ ☺ ☼

And so Ella, Aretta and I fell into a weird kind of friendship. We sat together whenever we were in the same class. We hung out at break and lunch times. Ella and I told Aretta stuff that had happened in our school before she came. Aretta told us all the things she could remember about life in Nigeria, when she was a little girl. She never talked about her life now, and Ella and I knew not to ask.

And every day, at four o'clock, Aretta disappeared out of our lives, with no explanation at all.

It was like being friends with Cinderella.

Chapter Fifteen

On Friday, Ella and I didn't even discuss a trip to the nursing home – we both just knew it was going to happen.

'And look what I brought,' I said when I arrived at her place, and unpacked the flask I'd sneaked from my kitchen. 'Now we won't have to take the kettle. I know Alyson isn't the most observant person in the world, but sooner or later even *she's* going to notice that the kettle is vanishing for a few hours every Friday night. Mum and Dad never use this flask though, so there's no chance they'll miss it.'

'Genius!' said Ella. 'Why didn't we think of

that before?'

When we got to Gigi's room, I could hear noises from inside. I pushed the door open and gasped. It was only a small room, but it was pretty much full. Gigi was there of course, and Fred and Nancy, and there were also two more old women propped up on the bed with their arms folded, and in the corner was a man in a wheelchair.

Gigi shrugged her thin shoulders. 'What could I do?' she asked. 'Word gets around.'

Ella and I looked at each other. How had one sneaky visit to her granny turned into a weekly party for half the residents of the nursing home?

'Can I cuddle Lucky?' asked Nancy. 'I've been looking forward to this all week.'

'Oh, Nancy, please could I hold her first?' asked one of the new ladies, reaching out with thin, old arms. 'I had to give my kitty away when I moved here three years ago, and I haven't touched an animal since.'

I think that might be the saddest thing I've ever heard. I quickly unwrapped Lucky from my fleece and handed her to Ella.

'You pass the baby around,' I said. 'And I'll get on with the tea.'

Luckily the flask I'd brought was huge, and I'd filled it right to the top.

'We didn't bring enough cups,' I said in a fake cross voice. 'Who knew that everyone who lives on this floor would be here, Gigi?'

Gigi laughed. 'Oh, not everyone's here. I invited them all, but Mary had to go to hospital, and Hannah's gone to stay with her daughter tonight. Michael, who is at the end of the corridor, is a bit of a fuddy-duddy. He wouldn't leave his room even if we told him The Beatles were playing a concert on my bed. Anyway, we'll manage if you get the water glasses from my bathroom.'

The man in the wheelchair gave a big wheezy

laugh. 'No need for that, girleen,' he said. 'I smuggled some cups from the dining room at supper-time.'

He pulled back the rug that was covering his knees to reveal four white mugs and a huge plate full of sandwiches.

'You naughty boy, Paddy!' said Nancy, and he laughed again, like it was the best thing anyone had said to him for weeks.

We all had tea and sandwiches, and the old people passed Lucky around. Lucky was very good, and seemed to be enjoying all the attention.

'This is really quite cool,' I was saying to Ella. 'I'm glad so many people—'

Just then an old lady stood up and headed for the door.

'You're not being fair,' she said in a sulky voice. 'Hannah has had three turns at holding Lucky, and I've only had one. I'm leaving.'

I half-stood up, wondering if I should try

to stop her, but Gigi shook her head at me. 'Peggy's just a drama queen,' she whispered. 'Let her alone, and she'll be fine in the morning.'

While this was happening, no one noticed Fred shuffling over to the table in the corner and picking up the flask.

'Maybe there's one last drop left....' he said.

Even though it was empty, the flask was too heavy for his twisted, old hands. It slipped from his fingers and landed on Lucky's tail. The poor dog yelped, and ran for the door, which Peggy had left open.

'OMG,' said Ella. 'Catch her, or we're all dead.'

'OK,' I said, running for the door. 'You stay here and keep everyone calm.'

As I turned the corner, I saw the tip of Lucky's tail disappearing down the stairs.

'Oh no!' I whispered. 'You silly dog. Don't go down there. That's where Nurse Witch is going to be.'

I raced down the stairs as quickly and quietly as I could manage. When I got to the ground floor, I peeped around the corner. All seemed quiet at the reception desk, and I could see Nurse Witch's shadow reflected on the floor, like an evil black puddle.

'Where are you, Lucky?' I whispered. 'Come back or you're going to get us all into a whole lot of trouble.'

And then I heard a quivery voice from a half-open door at the end of the corridor – a quivery voice saying two words that made my blood turn to ice.

'Nice doggie.'

The shadow didn't move, and I guessed that Nurse Witch was too far away to have heard. I legged it down the corridor, and slipped into the room, pulling the door closed behind me.

A small night-light gave the room a creepy red glow. In the corner, a woman was sitting up in bed, hugging Lucky, who was licking her face.

'Nice doggie,' said the woman again. 'Nice doggie.'

I didn't want to frighten her, so I walked very slowly over to the bed, and sat on the chair beside her.

'I'm Eva,' I said.

The old woman held Lucky with one hand, and reached the other hand towards me. I shook it, but it was like shaking a warm dry bundle of twigs, and I was half-afraid I'd hurt her.

'I'm Eleanor,' she said. 'And I'm very pleased to meet you. I don't get many visitors – and a visitor with a dog, why that's a very special treat indeed.'

She stroked Lucky, who cuddled up against the old lady's soft nightie, and closed her eyes.

It was a sweet moment, but I couldn't

enjoy it. All I could think was that, at any moment, Nurse Witch could march in, and then everything would be ruined.

'Oh,' I said, looking at an imaginary watch on my wrist. 'Is that the time? I'm afraid I must go now. I have to take Lucky home to bed.'

Eleanor didn't say anything, but as I reached out my hands, she lifted Lucky and held her towards me.

'Thank you,' I whispered, hardly daring to believe my luck.

The old lady lay down again.

'Good night,' I whispered.

'Good night, Madeleine,' she said. 'Thank you for coming.'

She gave a small smile and closed her eyes. I didn't have time to wonder who Madeleine was, or why she might be running around a nursing home in the middle of the night with a dog under her arm. I tip-toed out

of the room, and along the corridor. Nurse
Witch still hadn't stirred, so I cuddled
Lucky close to me and ran up the stairs.

It was turning into a very long night.

Chapter Sixteen

When I got into Gigi's room with Lucky, I was greeted like I'd just come back from a six-month expedition to the Arctic Circle. All the old people said stuff like 'well done' and 'clever girl' and a few of them even started to clap.

'Shhh,' I said, laughing in spite of all the stress. 'Nurse Witch will hear, and if she discovers us, Ella and I won't be able to visit next week.'

That made everyone fall silent. I was glad about that, but kind of sad too. Why were all these grown-ups so timid and obedient?

And then, as if she could read my mind –
again – Gigi stood up.

'Why are we all so afraid of Nurse Witch?'
she asked, waving her fist in the air.

'She's just an evil old spoilsport,' said Nancy.

'Hear, hear,' said Fred, rattling his walking
frame on the ground. 'We shouldn't let her
treat us the way she does. We might be old and
doddery but we still deserve to be treated with
dignity and respect.'

'We should tell Nurse Witch exactly what
we think,' said one of the new ladies. 'After all,
what can she do to us? She can't hurt us.'

She was right of course, but I was suddenly
scared.

Was it right for me to encourage these
people to rebel, when I was half-afraid of
Nurse Witch myself?

What if they spoke out and ended up
making things even worse than before? They'd
have to live with the results, while Ella and I

could skip off to our lovely homes. That totally wouldn't be fair.

Then Gigi sat down. 'Maybe we're getting a bit carried away,' she said. 'It's late, and we're all tired. Why don't we just go to bed? Tomorrow is a new day.'

I didn't know what to say. Had I just witnessed the shortest revolution in world history?

There was a second's silence and then the old people began to move. They made their way slowly to the door, whispering their goodbyes as they went.

Gigi climbed in to bed, and while I wrapped Lucky in my fleece, Ella gently tucked the bedclothes around her granny.

'Good night, Gigi,' she said. 'Don't let the bed-bugs bite.'

'Good night, Darling,' said Gigi. 'You've made everything different. Everything is better when you two are here.'

Ella kissed her granny, and then she switched off the light and we tip-toed from the room.

☽   ☺   ☼

When we got to the bottom of the stairs, we could see Nurse Witch sitting at her station. Her back was straight and she was all alert, like she knew that someone, somewhere was doing something wrong.

'Oh, no,' said Ella. 'It's getting late. If she doesn't move soon, we'll never get home before Mum and Dad. If they find out what we've been doing, we're dead – totally dead.'

'Maybe your parents will understand that we were just trying to help Gigi?'

'No way. All they'll understand is that I broke their rules, and I'll be grounded for weeks.'

I hugged Lucky even closer to me. If Ella got grounded, my life wasn't going to be a whole lot of fun either.

Just then there was the sound of a bell ringing, and Nurse Witch jumped up. Ella and I ducked back as she marched past. When she was safely gone, I peeped around the corner, just in time to see Nurse Witch disappearing into Eleanor's room.

'What is it, Eleanor?' I could hear her saying. 'It's very late, and you should be asleep.'

'I want to see the doggie,' said Eleanor. 'He was a very nice doggie. Can he come back?'

'You've been dreaming,' said Nurse Witch. 'There's no dog here. As you well know, animals aren't allowed in the building.'

'But he was here,' said Eleanor. 'I'm sure of it. And there was a lovely girl too. She said ...'

I wanted to hear the rest of the conversation, but Ella was pulling my arm.

'We've got to go,' she whispered.

I knew she was right. We escaped from the nursing home, dropped Lucky back to Maggie's house, and let ourselves in the back door of Ella's place.

Just as we were about to take off our jackets and boots, we heard the sound of Ella's dad's key in the front door.

'Quick,' whispered Ella. I raced up the stairs after her, and shoved the rucksack into a cupboard. There was no time to change. Without switching on the light, we both jumped into Ella's big double bed and pulled the covers up to our chins. A second later, Ella's mum was at the bedroom door.

'Are you asleep, girls?' she whispered.

'Sort of,' said Ella, in a fake sleepy voice.

Her mum crossed the room and sat on the end of the bed. I hoped she wouldn't notice that, under the covers, Ella and I still had our boots on.

'Well, I just came to tuck you in and say good-night,' she said, leaning over to stroke Ella's face.

'Oh, my goodness,' she said. 'Are you all

right, Ella? Your skin is ice cold. And what about you, Eva? Are you cold too?'

I shook my head, trying not to laugh. 'No,' I said. 'I'm fine, thanks. Just a bit sleepy.'

Luckily Ella's mum took the hint. 'Oh well,' she said. 'I'll put the heating on for an hour and maybe we need to get you a warmer blanket for your bed, Ella.'

'Yay,' said Ella, forgetting that she was supposed to be sleepy. 'There are totally cool fluffy ones in Daly's. Maybe we should get two, just to be on the safe side. I'd like a purple and a black one, and maybe a few cushions to complete the look.'

'You girls!' said her Mum.

She went out, closing the door behind her, and that was the end of another Friday night.

Chapter Seventeen

On Monday, it was lovely and sunny so Ella and I had our lunch on our favourite bench in the farthest corner of the playground.

'I'm kind of worried about Aretta,' I said as I unwrapped my lunch.

'Why?' asked Ella, leaning across to see what was in my sandwiches. 'Oh, chicken – lucky you. Want to swap for my cheese and tomato?'

I don't much like chicken sandwiches, so we swapped.

'Anyway,' said Ella through a mouthful of my sandwich. 'I haven't seen Aretta all morning. Why are you worried about her?'

'She's in my geography class, and she was already at her desk when I got there. At first I thought she was reading her geography book, but then I noticed that it wasn't even open. I asked her if she was OK, and she said she was, but she didn't sound at all OK. She sounded really upset.'

'Poor Aretta. What did you do?'

'I know we agreed not to talk to her about personal stuff, but I couldn't just say nothing. I asked her if she wanted to talk.'

'And?'

'She didn't say anything for ages, and I was starting to think she hadn't heard me, but then she looked up and I saw that her eyes were all red.'

'She'd been crying?'

'That's what it looked like. 'Whatever's wrong, you can tell me,' I said, and for a second, it looked like she was getting ready to talk, but then the teacher came in and started going on about some stupid geography test, and we couldn't talk any more.'

'And what happened after class?'

'Aretta disappeared, and I haven't seen her since. I feel like she was ready to talk to me, and now the opportunity has gone.'

'Well maybe you're going to get another opportunity,' said Ella. 'Look who's coming.'

Aretta was walking towards us. Her eyes weren't red any more, but she looked sad and tired.

I slid across the bench to make room and she sat down between Ella and me.

'Hey, Aretta,' said Ella. 'Do you want one of Eva's sandwiches? They're totally delicious.'

Aretta shook her head. 'No, thanks. I'm not hungry.' Her voice was so quiet, I could just about hear her.

I put my hand on her arm. 'I know you like to keep your personal stuff private, and I promise we're not trying to spy on you or anything, Aretta,' I said. 'But if there's something wrong, you know you can tell us.'

Aretta stared at me for a second and then she put her head in her hands. Ella and I looked at each other.

'We only want to help you,' said Ella.

'*No one* can help,' said Aretta from between her fingers.

'Try us,' I said.

'Eva's great at helping people,' said Ella. 'She's done all kinds of amazing things. I've told you before about how she saved Ruby's swimming trials, but there's lots more. Once she saved an ancient old tree from being cut down, and last year she solved a crime that had been a mystery for nearly a hundred years. Sometimes, when a problem is really big, only Eva can sort it out.'

I could feel myself going red. Ella's confidence in me was nice, but I didn't want Aretta to have false hopes. It's not like I can work miracles.

'And even if we can't help,' continued Ella. 'Just talking about stuff might make you feel better.'

Aretta looked up again.

'Can I tell you about my life?' she said.

'Sure,' said Ella, and I nodded in agreement. Somehow I knew this wasn't going to be a funny story about the cool things Aretta used to do with her mum in Nigeria.

'Like I told you before,' Aretta began. 'Eight years ago I came to Ireland with my dad and my brother, and at first we lived in Kilkenny.'

'Kilkenny's nice,' I said. 'We went there once on a school tour.'

Ella nudged me and I stopped talking. Aretta probably didn't want to hear about my day-trip to Kilkenny.

'Sorry,' I said. 'Go on.'

Aretta gave a tiny smile. 'My school in Kilkenny was great. I told you about the basketball already, but we played loads of other sports too. I made lots of really nice friends, but ...'

'Go on,' said Ella, in a gentle voice.

'Because we were asylum seekers, we had to live in a direct provision centre.'

'Like the one you live in now?' I said.

'Not exactly. We are guests in this country, and we are grateful for what we get, but ...'

There was a long silence, and I began to wonder if Aretta had changed her mind about confiding in us. Then she spoke in a big rush.

'The direct provision centre in Kilkenny was really, really awful. The manager, Mr Richards, treated us like we were animals. Whole families had to live in one tiny bedroom, and these rooms were too cold in winter and too warm in summer. We had no facilities to cook our own meals. We had to eat in a big ugly hall that always smelled bad, like rotten vegetables. The food was nasty, as if the manager deliberately picked things we wouldn't like.'

'So why did you stay?' I asked.

Aretta shrugged. 'We didn't have any choice. It's not like we could move up the road to a five star hotel or a fancy penthouse apartment. We had to stay with the horrible Mr Richards.'

'That all sounds awful,' said Ella.

'It was,' said Aretta. 'But we learned to put up with it. My father told my brother and me that we would have to be patient. One day our application to stay in Ireland will be accepted, he said, and then our lives will change forever. When my brother and I couldn't sleep, our father sat on our beds and told us stories of the lovely house we would all live in when we left the centre. He told us about the garden he would make for us, with swings and a little pond for fish. He said that one day, our mother would come and live with us there, and we would all be happy again.'

I could feel tears coming to my eyes. I

looked at Ella, but she was rubbing her face, like dust had blown on it or something. Aretta wasn't crying though. Her face was still and sad.

'As my brother got older, he didn't want to listen to those stories any more. He was angry all the time, and he fought with my father a lot. It was not easy, sharing a bedroom with those too, I can tell you. And then ...'

There was another long silence. I didn't want to rush her, but lunch-time was nearly over, and I had a funny feeling that if Aretta didn't finish her story before the bell rang, then she might never finish it.

'And then what?' I said as gently as I could.

'And then something terrible happened.' Now Aretta's voice was almost a whisper, like what she was describing was still happening in a hidden corner of her mind.

'It was dinner-time, the worst time of the day. There was a woman sitting at the table near us, with her little girl. When the food came out, the woman said that she was very sorry, but she could not eat it, because of her religious beliefs. She very politely asked the woman who served the food if she and her little girl could have something else. And then Mr Richards came along and started screaming at her. He said the woman should have made her request before the food was cooked, and the woman said she did not have a chance, because her little girl was sick. And then ... and then ... and then my brother jumped up, and before my father could do anything about it, my brother punched Mr Richards in the face. My brother is not very good at punching, and I don't think Mr Richards was really hurt, but he acted like he was going to die. He screamed and shouted and said he would have my brother locked up for twenty years.'

'But that's so unfair,' I said. 'It sounds like Mr Richards was totally mean to that woman.

He's the one who should be locked up.'

Aretta nodded. 'In the end Mr Richards calmed down. I think he knew he might get into trouble too – because he's supposed to provide special food for people who have strict religious beliefs. So he made a big fuss about how forgiving he could be. He said that if my family agreed to go back to Nigeria, he wouldn't call the police or bring charges against my brother.'

'But you didn't go back to Nigeria,' I said.

'No. We couldn't. For one thing, going back would be dangerous for us, and also ... well, I've been here for so long, I think I'm more Irish than Nigerian now. Those stories I tell you about Nigeria – well, they're just stories my dad has told me. Sometimes I feel like he made them all up. I've been here for most of my life, and going back – well, going back would be like going to a foreign country.'

'So how did you end up here?' asked Ella.

'One of the social workers was really nice. She found us a place here, but my brother refused to come with us. He went to Dublin to stay in a different centre, with his girlfriend and her family.'

I don't have any brothers or sisters, but even so, I guessed it must be hard to be parted from the only one you had.

Ella seemed to read my mind. 'You must miss your brother,' she said.

'I do,' said Aretta. 'But even so, I thought the move here might be a good thing. It meant we would be far away from Mr Richards.'

'And is the centre here better?' I asked.

Aretta nodded. 'It isn't perfect, but mostly it's OK. The building looks like it's about to fall down, but the people who work there are nice. The manager treats us well. The only problem is……'

Before she could finish, the bell rang to tell us that lunch-time was over. I felt like crying.

This was like my mum telling me to put away my book when it's time to go to sleep – only a million times worse.

Ella jumped up. 'Sorry, guys,' she said. 'But Mr Dean's on the warpath. If he catches us here when we should be on the way to class, we'll be in after-school detention for a week.'

She was right. And even though after-school detention wouldn't be much fun for Ella or me, it would be even worse for Aretta who was always gone from school about three seconds after the last bell rang.

As we stood up, a sudden gust of wind caught the wrappings from Ella's sandwiches and they flew through the air.

'Quick, Eva, help me,' shouted Ella. 'If we're caught littering, we'll get double detention.'

I raced after her, and when we came back with the scraps of paper, Aretta was already gone.

'Poor Aretta,' said Ella as we hurried back to class. 'Imagine having all those terrible things happen to you.'

'Yeah,' I said. 'It's totally awful, but still, I don't get what's going on.'

'What do you mean?'

'Well, Aretta was kind of ok last week, and the week before, but today she's all red-eyed and sad.'

'She's probably missing her mum and her brother.'

'But they've been gone all the time.'

'Maybe it's just sunk in,' said Ella. 'Like delayed shock or something.'

'No,' I said. 'That can't be it. She wouldn't have changed so quickly. Something else must have happened – and I think she'd have told us about it if the bell hadn't rung right in the middle of her story.'

'Yeah, maybe you're right. We'll have to try double-hard to catch her after school, and give her a chance to tell us what's going on.

☺ ☺ ☼

But, once again, Aretta managed to leave school without us seeing her. I met Ella at the gate, and she shook her head.

'I don't know how she does it,' she said. 'It's like she puts on an invisibility cloak once four o'clock comes.'

'Exactly,' I said. 'Anyway, we can talk to her tomorrow at lunch time, and once we find out what's going on, we can figure out a way of helping her.'

But Aretta didn't come to school the next day or any other day that week. Ella and I were totally worried about her, but we didn't dare to go to the detention centre to find out what was going on.

There was nothing we could do.

☽ ☺ ☼

That night my friend Kate FaceTimed me. (Kate lives in Seacove, where I go on holidays with my family. At first I thought she was totally weird, but when I got to know her, I realised that she's really, really nice. The only problem now is that she lives so far away I hardly ever get to see her.)

'Hey,' I said. 'It's so good to hear from you. How are you?'

She told me all the latest news from her school, and laughed a lot when I told her about how Ella and I sneaked Lucky into the nursing home to visit Gigi.

'So how's your adorable baby brother?' I said then.

She gave a huge, soppy smile. 'Simon is the cutest baby in the world,' she said. 'He knows loads of words now, and every day he learns more. He comes into my bed every morning to wake me up, and even if I'm really tired, his giggling makes me smile. When he laughs, he makes everything funny. He's just so …'

She stopped talking.

'What?' I said. 'What's wrong?'

'Sometimes when I think about how much I love Simon … it scares me to think that if it weren't for you, I might never even have known that he existed.'

I hoped my red face didn't show up on her screen. 'I didn't really—'

'You were amazing, Eva,' she said. 'You fixed my life. You made everything perfect again. You…..'

Now I was totally embarrassed. 'Yeah, well,' I said. 'Thanks for that, but I think I've lost my touch. There's a new girl called Aretta in my school. She's got *loads* of problems, and I can't think of a single way to help her.'

'That's so awful,' said Kate, when I'd finished telling her about Aretta. 'But don't worry. I know you'll be able to figure something out.'

I shook my head. 'I'm not so sure. I think this problem might be too big for me.'

'*No* problem is too big for you. Just do what you always do.'

'What's that?'

'Wait until the perfect idea comes to you, and then don't hang around worrying about if it's stupid, or if it's going to work – just go ahead and do it.'

We chatted for another while and then Kate had to go and do her homework.

Suddenly I realised how much I missed her.

'When are we going to see each other?' I asked. 'The holidays are ages away, and my mum and dad are really busy these days, so they don't have time to drive me to Seacove for just a day trip.'

Now Kate looked sad, and I felt sorry. 'Oh don't worry,' I said. 'We'll think of something.'

She gave a small smile. 'I guess. Now, I've

really got to go. Bye.'

I looked at the blank screen for ages. Kate is one of my best friends, and never seeing her is totally, totally unfair.

Chapter Eighteen

'**B**e brave, Lucky,' I whispered as we tip-toed up the stairs on Friday night. 'You've got a long night of cuddling ahead.'

'Yip, yip,' said Lucky.

Ella giggled. 'I wonder if that's doggie-speak for '*Yay!!* or *Please don't do this to me.*'

'We'll never know!' I said. 'Now hurry up, before Nurse Witch catches us.'

Once again, Gigi's room was full of people. The small table was set up with cups and saucers and plates full of sweets and biscuits.

'Oh, there you are girls,' said Gigi when she

saw us. 'Welcome to the party. I think you know everyone except for Hannah.'

She pointed to a small woman who was sitting in the corner of the room, knitting furiously.

'Hello, girls,' said Hannah, without looking up. 'I'm so excited to be here. My daughter invited me to visit her this weekend, but I said no. Her house is very boring compared to the parties here on Friday night. Now can you pass Lucky to me, I want to see if this coat I'm knitting for her is big enough yet?'

'Where's Peggy?' I asked, remembering the woman who had marched off the week before.

'She didn't want to come,' said Gigi. 'She's sulking again. Paddy rolled over her foot at breakfast this morning, and Peggy said he did it deliberately.'

'I *did* do it deliberately,' said Paddy. 'She took the last slice of toast.'

I started to laugh, but stopped when I

realised he wasn't joking. Then I felt worried.

'Peggy seems to be a bit of a troublemaker,'
I whispered to Ella. 'What if she decides to tell
Nurse Witch about our Friday night parties?
Maybe we should ask Gigi what she thinks.'

'No,' said Ella. 'Everyone's having such a
lovely time. Let's not worry them. Let's just
cross our fingers and hope that Peggy hasn't got
a mean streak.'

☽   ☺   ☼

Twenty minutes later, the party was going
great. Nancy was organising strict five-minute
hugging sessions with Lucky, Gigi was pouring
the last of the tea, and Fred was passing around
plates of food. And then Gigi's bedroom door
was pushed open, and Peggy hurried in.

'Nurse Witch is coming!' she said.

'You told on us!' said Paddy. 'You wicked
woman. I knew you didn't have a decent bone
in your body.'

'No,' wailed Peggy. 'I told no one.'

'But it's only half-past ten,' said Fred. 'Why would Nurse Witch be coming up now?'

'I was just coming in to say hello,' said Peggy, 'when I saw the call-light over Michael's door come on.'

Gigi had told us about the man at the end of the corridor who never left his room. If he had pressed his call button, then we only had a few minutes before Nurse Witch came along the corridor. I pictured her putting her book down with a big sigh, and slowly making her way up the stairs.

'Maybe she won't come in here,' said Ella. 'Maybe if we're all really quiet, everything will be fine.'

'It's not going to be fine,' said Gigi, shaking her head. 'Nurse Witch rarely comes up here, but when she does, she checks in every bedroom.'

'We're doomed,' said Peggy. 'We're all doomed.'

'No, we're not,' said Nancy. 'Everyone hide.'

That was a good idea, except that there were eight people and a dog in the room, and the only places to hide were the teeny-tiny bathroom, and a cupboard that looked like it was made to hold dolls' clothes.

And then Gigi stood up. 'I'm not hiding,' she said. 'Last time I checked, we were all adults.'

'I'm not an adult,' said Ella.

'Nor me,' I said. 'And Lucky's only six months old. Even in dog years, she's pretty much a baby.'

'Then maybe it's better if you three hide,' said Gigi, pushing us towards the bathroom. 'Or else things might get a bit complicated. But I am going to stand my ground. Who's with me?'

As I grabbed Lucky and followed Ella in to the bathroom, I heard a big defiant chorus from the bedroom.

'We're all with you,' said Paddy. 'Every last one of us. We'll fight this to the death.'

'Maybe not that far,' said an old lady. 'I like being alive.'

'Leave the door open a tiny bit,' I whispered to Ella. 'I don't want to miss a second of this.'

'I don't think I can bear to look.'

'But isn't it so great to see Gigi and her friends standing up for themselves?'

'I guess,' said Ella. 'But what if it all goes horribly wrong?'

Chapter Nineteen

For a few minutes, the only sounds were the beating of my heart, and the dry coughing of one of the old ladies in the bedroom.

Next to me, Ella started to relax. 'Maybe everything's going to be OK. Maybe Nurse Witch checked on Michael and then went back downstairs.'

I shook my head. 'I doubt it. Gigi says she's like a machine, and machines don't think. They just do the same thing, over and over again. They always......'

I stopped talking as I heard the bedroom door being pushed open.

'Mrs Walker!' came Nurse Witch's angry voice. 'Why is your light on at this time of night? Why is…….?'

I peeped out and saw Nurse Witch standing in the doorway of the bedroom. Her face was white and angry.

'What on *earth* is going on here? Mr Edge, Mrs Parsons, why aren't you in your rooms? Don't you know the rules?'

Gigi and her friends were huddled together in the corner of the room, staring at the matron. They looked old and scared.

'The poor things,' whispered Ella. 'They want to stand up to her, but they're not brave enough.'

'Give them a chance,' I said, not really daring to hope.

'Well?' said Nurse Witch, walking further into the room, with a cruel smirk on her face. 'Has anyone got anything to say?'

And then Paddy wheeled his chair towards

Nurse Fitch, stopping just a centimeter from her ugly white shoes.

'Of course we haven't forgotten the rules,' he said. 'How could we? You've got them printed up and stuck to every surface in the place. For all I know, you've got them tattooed on your bottom.'

Nurse Witch looked like she was going to explode. Some of the old ladies gasped in horror, but Gigi stepped forwards, laughing loudly.

'Ha!' she said. 'Very funny, Paddy. I couldn't have put it better myself. The thing is, Nurse Fitch, we are all perfectly aware of your stupid rules. We have just decided that we're not going to follow them anymore.'

Peggy stepped forwards too. 'So what are you going to do about that, Nurse Fitch, or should I say, Nurse *Witch*?'

Now all the old people shuffled forwards, laughing like crazy.

Nurse Witch's mouth was wide open, but she didn't say anything. She took a few steps backwards.

'Ha!' said Hannah, waving her knitting needles a bit too close to Nurse Witch's face. 'You're like all bullies – a coward at heart.'

'Yesss!' I whispered. 'Go, Hannah.'

Peggy took another step forwards. 'My nephew is a journalist in the local newspaper. If you don't leave us alone, I might just tell him that this place is full of bed-bugs.'

Nurse Witch looked like she'd been slapped. 'You can't do that,' she said. 'Telling lies to the newspapers is a crime.'

Peggy laughed a big loud laugh. 'Ha! I'm ninety-eight and three quarters. What are they going to do to me? Send me to jail for life?'

But then Nurse Witch recovered a bit. Her voice was sharp and cold like early-morning frost. She took a notebook and pen from her uniform pocket, and began to write. 'I am recording all of your names,' she said.

'Ohhh, we're in the naughty notebook,' said Peggy, giggling like a bold schoolgirl. 'We're all scared now.'

'You *should* be scared,' said Nurse Witch. 'Because you are all now on a warning. If you don't start following the rules, I will be writing to your families to ask them to consider finding new homes for you.'

'You won't have to do that,' said Gigi. 'We're fed up of this place with its stupid rules and regulations. We're leaving anyway, aren't we?'

No one said anything for a second, and then there was a chorus of voices. 'Yes,' they said. 'We're leaving.'

'But Gigi can't leave,' I whispered to Ella. 'You said there aren't any other nursing homes near here. If she moves, she'll end up miles and miles away from your family and we'll never get to see her.'

But Ella was smiling. 'Gigi's bluffing,' she

said. 'We always play cards at Christmas and Gigi is a champion bluffer. Just you watch.'

For ages and ages, Gigi faced Nurse Witch with her arms folded. The only sound was the click-clack of Hannah's knitting needles.

And then Gigi spoke again. 'I wonder, Nurse, could you be so kind as to bring me the portable phone? I would like to call my son to make arrangements for my new residence.'

'And I want the phone after her,' said Peggy.

'Then me,' said Fred.

'I don't mind waiting till last,' said Hannah. 'I need to finish this row.'

And that's when Nurse Witch cracked. I guess she knew she'd be in trouble with the health board if half the residents of the nursing home decided to leave at the same time.

'Let's not be hasty here,' she said. 'Why don't we all sleep on this?'

'We can sleep when we're dead,' said Peggy.

'We're not sleeping until this is settled,'

said Gigi calmly. 'We don't want you showing up here in the morning with a pack of reinforcements.'

'So what exactly is it that you want?' asked Nurse Witch weakly.

'Ice-cream for tea every night,' said a woman I'd never heard speak before. 'And we want a choice of chocolate and raspberry ripple – and caramel sauce on Sundays.'

'Agreed,' said Nurse Witch. 'Now will you break up this party and go to bed?'

'Oh no!' I whispered. 'They finally stood up to her. Surely they're not going to let her away that easily? Did they do all this just for a few bowls of ice-cream?'

And then Gigi spoke. 'There's one more thing,' she said. 'You seem to forget that we are adults, not bold babies. It is wrong to expect us to stay in our rooms after eight o' clock. We demand that we be allowed to go wherever we like until midnight – or later if we so choose.'

After only a tiny hesitation, Nurse Witch nodded her head.

'Agreed.'

Before she could change her mind, Peggy pulled down the rule-sheet that was pinned just inside the door. She handed it to Nurse Witch.

'Rule 27,' she said. '*Barring emergencies, residents will remain in their rooms after 8.00pm.* We'd like you to cross that out now, and you can amend all the other notices in the building tomorrow.'

Slowly Nurse Witch took out her pen and crossed out rule 27.

'Happy?' she said.

'I'm not,' said the quiet woman. 'I won't be happy until you write in the ice-cream rule – and don't forget to mention the caramel sauce.'

Ella and I tried not to laugh out loud as Nurse Witch carefully added a line to the list of rules.

'Now,' she said. 'That's done. Will you please go back to your rooms?'

'We don't have to,' laughed Nancy. 'You've changed the rules. We can stay here all night if we want.'

Nurse Witch looked like she was going to cry, but then I guess Paddy felt sorry for her. 'I reserve my right to stay as long as I like, but it's been an exciting evening, and I'm a little tired. I think I'll go to bed. Thank you for a lovely evening, Gigi.'

He wheeled himself past Nurse Witch and out of the room, followed by the rest of the party-goers. Nurse Witch was the last to leave. She didn't say anything, as she closed the door hard behind her.

⌣ ☺ ☼

'OMG!' said Ella as she raced out and hugged her granny. 'That was so cool. I thought Nurse Witch was going to die.'

I hugged Gigi too. 'Well done,' I said. 'You were brilliant. You were all brilliant. Life's going to be much nicer around here from now on because you were brave enough to stand up to that bully.'

Gigi smiled. 'Thank you dear. Now, let me cuddle Lucky one more time, and then I think I will retire. It's long past my bedtime.'

☽ ☺ ☼

As soon as Gigi was tucked up in bed, Ella and I tip-toed down the stairs. Nurse Witch was behind the reception desk, talking on the phone.

'Let's hope she doesn't chat for too long,' said Ella. 'We need to get out of here.'

'Shhh,' I said, as I tip-toed closer. 'I wonder what she's talking about.'

We stopped at the corner just a metre or two away from the desk, and settled down to listen.

'Oh, Mammy,' said Nurse Witch. 'I thought

this job would be easier than being in the army, but it's not. I thought old people would like rules and regulations – I thought a strict regime would make them feel secure, but that's not the case at all. Oh, Mammy, I'd sooner go into battle against tanks and guns than ever again face that man in his wheelchair and the old woman with the knitting needles. Oh Mammy, what am I going to do at all?'

Beside me, Ella was laughing madly. 'Oh, Mammy, she mocked. 'I think I'm going to die from laughing.'

'But don't you feel the *teensiest* bit sorry for Nurse Witch?' I said. 'Clearly she's in the wrong job.'

Now Ella was serious. 'I don't care if she's in the wrong job, she upset my granny, and *no one* gets away with that.'

Chapter Twenty

XoXo

On Monday, Ella and I were doing our usual lunch time sandwich swap when Aretta appeared.

'Hey,' I said as she sat down between us. 'Where've you been?'

'We were worried about you,' said Ella.

'I'm OK,' said Aretta in a voice that seemed to be saying the opposite.

'So where were you last week?' I asked again.

'I was sick,' she said. 'That's the problem with living in a crowded place – sickness spreads quickly.'

'I'm glad you're better,' I said. 'But before

you left last week, we were having a chat, remember?'

Aretta sighed. 'You're not going to give up and talk about the weather are you?'

I grinned. 'No.'

'You were starting to tell us about where you live now,' said Ella.

'Yes,' said Aretta. 'That.'

'You'd got to the part with the "but,"' I said.

'Yes,' said Aretta again. 'It's not the worst place I've ever lived in, but ... the problem is my father.'

'OMG,' I said. 'Is he sick or something?'

'No,' said Aretta. 'Well, his body isn't sick, but he's sad all the time.'

He's far from home and from his wife and his son, I thought. *No wonder he's sad.*

It was as if Aretta could read my mind. 'Of course he was sad before, but not like this. When we were in Kilkenny, my father had sad moments, but then he'd get over them, and be positive again. He always looked forward to a bright future for us, but now he's different.'

'How exactly?' asked Ella.

'It's hard to explain ... it's like the sadness is eating into his bones, and it's getting worse and worse. I haven't seen him smile for weeks. Some of the other people in the centre are really nice, but my father doesn't even try to make friends with them. All he does is sit in his room and look at the wall. He won't talk to anyone except me.'

Suddenly I had a light-bulb moment. 'So that's why you rush off every evening after school?'

She nodded. 'I'm sorry I lied to you both. I wasn't at after-school classes; even if I had the money for fancy ballet or music lessons, I couldn't join up. When I'm not with him, my father has nothing to do, so after school, I go home as quickly as I can. I sit in his room and we talk about my brother and my mother and the home we used to have in Nigeria.'

That didn't sound like much fun for either of them. I tried to imagine the poor girl spending every evening with her sad and lonely father.

Then I remembered something. 'Last week,' I said. 'Your eyes were all......you looked a bit ... well ... you looked ... very upset.'

Aretta nodded. 'Recently my father has been especially bad. It is like he has lost all hope. When I got home from school some days, I could tell that he had been crying.'

I've only seen my dad cry once. It happened not long after he lost his job. Until then, I believed that my dad could fix everything, and when it turned out that he couldn't, it was really, really scary.

I gave Aretta a quick hug. 'I'm sorry,' I said. 'We had no idea what was going on. No wonder you were so mad when we followed you home.'

'What can we do to help?' asked Ella.

Aretta shrugged. 'I don't know. There are social workers at the centre, but how can they help us when my father won't even talk to them?'

'My father lost his job a few years ago,' I said. 'And he was very sad for a while.'

'Maybe we could help your father to find a job?' suggested Ella.

'A job would change everything,' said Aretta. 'My father is a very proud man, and he likes to be busy. The only problem is, because of our legal status, my father isn't allowed to work.'

'But that's stupid,' I said. 'What's he supposed to do all day? What are all the adults at the centre supposed to do?'

'We children are the lucky ones,' said Aretta. 'We are allowed to go to school, and mix with the local people. For the adults it is much harder. For them there is nothing.'

'Maybe you could arrange a surprise trip to Dublin for your dad,' I said. 'So he could visit your brother?'

'We have no money for trips anywhere,' said Aretta. 'Our weekly allowance doesn't even pay for essentials.'

I felt around in my pocket, wondering if a twenty euro note had magically appeared there, but I was disappointed to find only ten cents and a dirty tissue. 'Anyway,' Aretta continued. 'That is a nice thought, but even if we could persuade him to go, a trip to Dublin wouldn't really fix anything. My father would be happy for a day, but afterwards, I fear he would be worse than ever.'

'Your father needs a purpose in life,' said Ella. 'My granny, Gigi, always says that if you don't have a reason to get up in the morning, then your life is over.'

'She sounds like a wise woman,' said Aretta.

I pictured Gigi with her wild hair and crazy clothes and wondered if Aretta was right.

Just then the bell for the end of lunch-time

rang, and before I could say another word, Aretta grabbed her stuff and ran back in to school.

☺ ☺ ☼

'How's your new friend these days?' asked Dad that night.

'And when are you going to bring her over to meet us?' asked Mum.

'Probably never,' I said, and then I went on to tell them what I knew about Aretta and her dad.

'The poor girl,' said Mum. 'That's really hard on her.'

'I know,' I said. 'It's all so unfair. Her dad really wants to work, but he's not allowed to. Why do there have to be so many stupid rules?'

'It's hard to say,' said Dad. 'I expect when the rule was made, it made perfect sense to someone.'

'Well it makes *no* sense to me,' I said. 'I wonder if I could start a campaign to have that rule changed?'

Mum smiled. 'That's very sweet of you, Eva,' she said. 'But—'

'Why does there have to be a 'but'?' I said. 'Remember how our campaign saved the tree that was so special to Kate?'

'That was truly amazing, Eva,' said Dad. 'But this is a slightly different situation. Rules like this *can* be changed, but it takes many years. I'm afraid this problem isn't going to be fixed any time soon.'

'That's so pathetic,' I said. 'When I'm old enough to vote, I'm never going to vote for people who make stupid rules just to annoy people. And I *am* going to help Aretta. I'm just not sure yet how I'm going to do it.'

Mum hugged me. 'That's my girl,' she said. 'Why don't you sleep on it? Everything is clearer after a good night's sleep.'

But the next morning, I still wasn't any closer to a solution. When I got to school I met Aretta in the corridor. I thought about telling her that I'd been thinking about her all night, but that sounded a bit weird.

'Hey,' I said instead. 'How are things? How's your dad?'

She shrugged. 'Just the same, I guess. I hate leaving him every morning. He just stands at the door and watches me walk away.'

'That's so sad,' I said.

'We talked for a long time last night. He told me all about the last work he did before we left Nigeria.'

'Hadn't he ever told you about it before?'

She gave a small smile. 'Only about a million times. I don't mind listening again, but that story always makes him especially sad. My father says that his last project was the best one he ever did – and now he is afraid he will never work again.'

Ella came up beside us, and heard Aretta's last words. 'Hey,' she said. 'You never did tell us what your dad's job was.'

'He designed and built gardens, and he was really, really good at it. He could take the smallest, ugliest patch of ground and turn it into a magical place.'

'That sounds cool,' I said. 'And what was his last project? The one he was talking about last night?'

'That was so amazing,' said Aretta. 'It was a special garden for a visually impaired boy. There were all kinds of things for him to smell, and touch and listen to.'

'That sounds so cool,' I said.

'It was totally cool,' said Aretta. 'And that's why it makes my dad so sad. He is afraid that he will never make a garden like it again. He says that he is forgetting all of his landscaping skills. His ideas are becoming old and rusty. He says ...'

But I wasn't listening any more. I'd just had an amazing idea.

☽ ☺ ☼

'Do we have to do this right now?' asked Ella that afternoon. 'I've got a project to finish, and Mum's giving me a hard time about the state of my bedroom.'

I smiled to myself as I remembered Kate's words – 'Just go ahead and do it.'

'Sorry, Ella,' I said. 'This needs to be done now – but I'll give you a hand with your project later if you like. Now can you walk a bit faster? There's no time to waste.'

'It's not Friday,' said Maggie as she opened the door. 'And it's not the middle of the night.'

Ella and I followed her into the kitchen, and sat at the table while Maggie poured out glasses of lemonade, and Lucky ran around in excited yappy circles beside us.

'So to what do I owe this honour?' asked Maggie as she put the glasses in front of us.

'We just thought it would be nice to see you,' I said, a bit pathetically.

Maggie rolled her eyes. 'I know you, Eva Gordon,' she said. 'You're a lovely girl, but there's always an agenda.'

Ella giggled. I didn't know if I should be insulted or flattered.

'OK,' I said. 'You've found me out. I've been thinking about your garden.'

'What about it?' asked Maggie.

'Well it's such a mess.'

'Thanks a lot,' said Maggie pretending to be hurt.

'You admitted it yourself,' I said. 'You said it was like a jungle. So I thought maybe we should do something about it.'

Maggie patted my arm. 'That's very sweet of you, Eva,' she said. 'But I'm afraid there are a few huge problems. I've seen those garden design programmes on TV, and while they look great, everything costs a fortune. My jewellery business is going well, but I don't have that kind of money.'

'I think we can get around that,' I said.

'And there's another problem too,' said Maggie. 'Even if you could magically get my garden made over, it wouldn't be fair to let you do it.'

'Why?' asked Ella. 'I think it sounds like a great idea.'

'Gardens need time and care,' said Maggie. 'I love gardening, and I could make time, but I can't take care of a garden. I can do lots of things in my wheelchair, but sadly, gardening isn't one of them. As you know, I can't even get my chair down the path any more. I'm afraid my gardening days are over.'

'But that's where you're wrong,' I said. 'I spent most of last night on the internet, and there are all kinds of things you can do to make your garden accessible. We can widen the paths, and build special raised beds, so you can reach them from your chair. We can......'

Maggie held up her hand. 'Please stop, Eva,' she said. 'This is a very sweet idea, but I think it's a bit ambitious. You are the most determined girl I know, but you are not a garden designer. Even if you spend six months on the internet, you won't be able to do this. You would need professional help.'

'Of course we need professional help, and I know exactly who's going to give it.'

'Who?' asked Maggie, not looking very hopeful.

'Remember our friend, Aretta – the one we gave the bracelet to? Well, her dad's a genius garden designer!'

'But I can't afford—'

Ella interrupted her. 'I don't think he'll take money.'

'I think it might even be against the law for him to take money,' I added. 'But this isn't about money, anyway. If you let this man design a garden for you, you'll be doing him a huge, huge favour. I think you might even change his life.'

And so Ella and I told Maggie all about Aretta and her dad, and when we were finished, Maggie was close to tears.

'That poor, poor man,' she said. 'If helping me will help him, then let's get started.'

'Yesss!' said Ella and I together.

Then Maggie stopped smiling. 'But who's going to do the work?' she said. 'And who's going to pay for the materials?'

I grinned. 'I've got a plan,' I said. 'You can leave it all to me.'

Chapter Twenty-one

'Guess what?' said Ella as we walked to school the next morning. 'The most amazing thing has happened. Gigi and her friends in the nursing home have formed a residents' committee.'

'And I'm guessing Gigi is the president?'

'Of course. And Paddy is her second-in-command. Yesterday they had a big formal meeting with Nurse Witch.'

'That's brilliant,' I said. 'And how did it turn out?'

'They reviewed all of her stupid rules, and managed to persuade her to change loads of them.'

'Wow,' I said. 'Good old Gigi.'

'Yeah, once she gets going, it's hard to stop her.'

'OMG,' I said. 'What about the no-pet rule? Did they manage to get rid of that?'

Ella shook her head.

'Unfortunately, that's the only thing that Nurse Witch wouldn't budge on. She said that if she allowed one person to visit with a kitten, the next person would want to bring a dog, and before she'd know it there would be donkeys and hyenas and miniature pigs fetching up on her doorstep.'

I giggled. 'Who knew Nurse Witch had a sense of humour?'

'I think she was being serious. It sounds like she was kind of afraid. Remember what she was like when Jessie went near her? She's obviously got a big thing against animals. I'm guessing she got bitten by a dog, or trodden on by an elephant when she was a kid.'

'That's not our problem,' I said. 'And why should the old people suffer just because of her phobias?'

'They shouldn't, but what can we do about it?'

'It's very simple,' I said. 'Animals are important to Gigi and her friends, and if Nurse Witch won't allow animals in, well we're just going to have to get rid of her.'

'You're kidding, right?'

I shrugged. 'Possibly. I'm not sure, yet.'

☺ ☺ ☼

At lunchtime, Ella and I told Aretta about our plan for Maggie's garden. When we'd finished, she had tears in her eyes, which was a bit embarrassing.

'All you have to do is get your father to go to Maggie's house,' I said. 'And then we can explain how he could help her by designing an accessible garden for her.'

'That's so sweet of you both,' she said. 'And I really, really appreciate it, but—'

'But what?' I asked. I was a bit disappointed by her reaction, because I thought it was a great plan – one of the best I'd ever had.

'But, my father is very, very sad all the time.'

'We *know*,' I said. 'That's why we came up with the plan. We want to give him something to do.'

'I understand that,' said Aretta. 'But the thing is, it is as if my father is hiding away from the world. Some days he barely gets out of bed. I don't think I will be able to persuade him to go to Maggie's house.'

'Does he *ever* leave the centre,' asked Ella.

'Very rarely,' sighed Aretta. 'He has only left once in the last month.'

'And what was that for?' I asked.

'He came to meet my science teacher. My father would do anything to help me to get a good education.'

'Well, don't say anything about meeting Maggie, then,' I said. 'Tell your dad it's a meeting about your education.'

'You want me to lie to him?'

'It won't be a lie,' I said. 'I've watched you. I know you spend most of the day worrying about your father, and that has to be a distraction. If your father continues the way he is, your education *is* going to suffer.'

'That's true,' said Aretta.

'Then it's sorted,' I said. 'Tell your dad you need him to do something to help your school-work. Be all vague about it, and when you get him out of the centre, we'll bring him to meet Maggie.'

'You think that'll work?' asked Aretta.

'Sure, it'll work,' I said. 'It's all sorted. Here, write down this address, and Ella and I will see you there at five o'clock this evening.'

'I can't help feeling bad about this,' said Maggie as we sat in her kitchen that afternoon. 'It's like I'm taking advantage of this poor man's situation.'

'That's absolutely not the case,' I said. 'Trust me, Maggie. If you let Aretta's father design a garden for you, you'll be doing him a huge favour – and if it happens to help you too, well then it's a win-win, and what's not to like about that?'

Before she could answer, the doorbell rang, and Ella ran to answer it.

She came back with a nervous-looking Aretta, who introduced us to her very embarrassed-looking father, who had to be wondering what he was doing standing in Maggie's kitchen.

Aretta's dad was a tall man with a thin, serious face. His clothes were worn and shabby and his shoes looked like something from an old-fashioned movie. We all shook hands and then there was a long silence. Everyone looked at me, like I was supposed to know what to do next.

'Er … it's really warm in here,' I said in the end. 'Why don't we go out to the garden for a bit?'

Even the people who were in on the plan looked at me like I was crazy, but I ignored them. I opened the back door and practically dragged Aretta and Ella outside. Aretta's dad politely stood back, so Maggie could wheel herself through the door, and then he followed.

'Not much room here,' I said brightly, as the five of us squashed together on the tiny patio. 'Why don't we all go down the garden a bit?'

Then I turned around, like I had just noticed that Maggie was there in her wheelchair.

'Oh, so sorry, Maggie,' I said. 'I forgot you

can't go past the patio. Isn't that a terrible pity? I couldn't imagine not being able to go down to the end of my very own garden.'

Ella rolled her eyes at me, but I just made a face at her. After all, it wasn't like she was rushing in with any amazing idea of her own.

But then Aretta's dad spoke for the first time. 'This path is too narrow for you,' he said to Maggie. 'It would not be difficult to make it wider so you could go to the end of the garden.'

'Yes, I …' began Maggie, but she stopped because Aretta's dad was walking away through the overgrown grass and shrubs. I thought he was being a bit rude, but then I saw that Aretta was smiling.

'OMG,' she said. 'Did you see that look on his face? I haven't seen that for weeks and weeks.'

'He looks really interested,' said Ella.

'Yeah,' I said. 'And with a bit of luck, Aretta,

he might even forget that you tricked him to get him here.'

We stood there for a bit, occasionally seeing Aretta's dad walking up and down the garden. In the end he came back to us.

'Could I trouble you for a pen and some paper?' he said politely to Maggie.

I ran in and grabbed an old notebook and a pencil from the kitchen table.

Aretta's dad took it from me and wandered back in to the jungle, with Lucky following at his heels, like she was going to have to protect him from wild animals.

'Don't worry,' I said. 'If you get lost, Lucky knows the way back.'

But Aretta's dad didn't turn around. He just kept on walking, like it was a matter of life or death.

'This is so amazing,' said Aretta as the rest of us went inside. 'I can't believe my father is doing something besides sitting around looking sad. I know this mightn't be a big deal to any of you guys, but to me it's like a miracle.'

Maggie squeezed my hand. 'Eva's our little miracle-worker,' she said, and I had to look away, so no one could see how embarrassed I was.

Twenty minutes later Aretta's dad came inside and sat next to Maggie at the kitchen table. He was all buzzy and excited.

'When I was in horticultural college in Nigeria,' he said. 'Everyone had to do a graduation project, and mine was a design of an accessible garden. I was proud of my work, but I never had the opportunity to use my ideas. That was many years ago, but I haven't forgotten them.'

He put a page in front of Maggie. 'This is very rough,' he said. 'But I think you can see what I would like to do. We can widen the paths and put the plants in raised beds and hanging baskets, all at a height suitable to you. We can build a barbecue that you can reach, and maybe a small fish-pond. We can make a kennel for Lucky. Do you need that shed for storage?'

'Not really,' said Maggie. 'There's just a few things in it.'

'Excellent,' said Aretta's dad. 'We can make a small storage box for the far corner of the garden where no one will see it, and we can adapt the shed to make a gazebo, where you can sit on the sunniest days.'

Maggie was laughing. 'This all sounds very ambitious,' she said.

Aretta's father laughed too. 'Ambition is good,' he said. 'It is important to have something to dream of. Now, would you allow me to draw up a proper plan for your garden?'

'I would *love* that,' said Maggie. 'But I have to make it clear that I can't afford to pay you for your work.'

Aretta's dad smiled at her. 'Payment is not always about money,' he said.

☺ ☺ ☼

At school the next morning, Aretta was smiling so much I thought her face was going to crack in two.

'My father barely slept last night,' she said. 'He spent hours on the ancient computer in the common room. He's already got the outline of the design drawn up, and when I left this morning, he was working on the smaller details.'

'That's so cool,' said Ella.

'It's *very* cool,' said Aretta. 'It's like it's been raining for months, and now the sun has come out. My father has come back to me.'

'That's brilliant news. I'm glad our plan worked out.'

'Oh,' said Aretta. 'There's one thing I need to ask you.'

'What?'

'Are you and Ella free after school? My father is going to the library to do some research this afternoon, so I thought maybe the three of us could hang out for a bit?'

'OMG!' I said as I hugged her. 'Cinderella is dead! Let's go.'

'Oh, no,' said Aretta. 'I can't go yet. I've just remembered something.'

'What?' I asked. Was she already changing her mind?

'I've got to go to sign up for after-school basketball,' she said. 'I'm going to start next week.'

'That's brilliant,' I said. 'I bet you'll be the star of the team.'

But then I remembered something too. 'Oh no!' I said. 'We've got heaps of maths homework, and it's going to take me hours. I have *no* idea how to do it.'

'I'll help you,' said Aretta. 'Maths is easy

when you know how.'

'Yay!' said Ella. 'A maths afternoon, Sounds like a whole pile of fun. Not.'

I giggled. 'Let's go to my place. With Aretta's help, my homework might not take that long. And afterwards we can watch a movie. How does that sound?'

'Perfect!' said Ella and Aretta together.

Chapter Twenty-two

'**I**'m going to die of the cold,' said Ella. (Or at least I think that's what she said. It was hard to be sure because her teeth were chattering so much.)

I tried to hug her, but hugging isn't easy when you've got a small, wriggly dog under your arm.

'This so isn't fair,' I said. 'Thanks to Gigi's committee, visitors are allowed until ten o'clock, but because of Lucky, we still have to hide outside like criminals.'

'I guess we just have to be patient,' said Ella. 'Nurse Witch *has* to move soon.'

But she didn't. It was like her bottom had been super-glued to her seat. Ella and I watched as she very slowly turned the pages of her book, occasionally sipping from her cup of tea.

I shivered. 'If we don't move soon, I'm going to get pneumonia and I'll end up in a nursing home myself.'

'You should have worn a coat,' said Ella primly, pulling hers up tighter around her neck.

I knew I couldn't take any more. 'Give me your coat,' I said, reaching out and tugging at the zip.

'Hey,' said Ella. 'Back off. You're not getting it.'

'It's not for me,' I said. 'It's for Lucky.'

'But Lucky's got her own personal fur coat.'

I laughed. 'She's not going to wear your coat. Just give it to me, Ell.'

And because Ella trusts me, she took off

her coat and passed it over. She watched as I wrapped Lucky in it and tucked her under my arm.

'See,' I said. 'The invisible dog.'

'I'm not sure …' she began, but I didn't wait to hear the rest. I was already marching up to the electronic keypad. I didn't look back, but behind me I could hear Ella's footsteps on the gravel. I smiled as I keyed in the code.

Nurse Witch looked up as we walked in to the reception.

'It's very late,' she said, like we couldn't read the huge clock over her head. 'Shouldn't children be in bed by now?'

'Oh, no,' I said. 'We're allowed to stay up late on weekend nights, aren't we, Ella?'

Ella didn't answer. She was staring at the bundle under my arm, like it was a bomb that could go off at any second.

'We're just going up to see Gigi, I said. 'We're so glad that you had the idea to change the visiting times.'

Nurse Witch tightened her mouth and glared at me. We both knew very well that the change in visiting hours hadn't been her idea.

'Oh, well,' I said. 'We can't hang around chatting. See you later.'

I was feeling very pleased with myself when, from under Ella's coat, came a very distinctive sound – Lucky's short, sharp bark.

'Yip, yip, yip.'

Nurse Witch jumped to her feet. 'What's that noise?' she said.

'What noise?' I asked innocently. 'Did you hear something, Ella?'

And then it came again.

'Yip. Yip.'

I held the bundle under my arm a bit tighter, silently begging Lucky to be good.

Nurse Witch picked up a crutch that was propped in the corner. She walked slowly around to our side of the desk, waving the crutch in front of her, like she was getting ready to fight off a pack of wolves.

And finally Ella came to life.

'Yip. Yip,' she said, sounding exactly like Lucky.

Nurse Witch stopped walking and stared at her suspiciously.

'Yip. Yip,' said Ella again. 'Yip. Yip. Yip. Yippety-yip.'

'Ella's got this funny syndrome,' I said thinking of a documentary my mum had been watching the week before. 'It's this thing where you can't help shouting out random stuff. Didn't you learn about it at nursing school, Nurse?'

Nurse Witch didn't answer.

'It can be totally embarrassing sometimes, can't it, Ella?' I said. 'Remember the time you ran down the street tearing out pages from your Maths copy and giving them to randomers?'

'Fart-bottom,' said Ella suddenly. 'Wee-wee face.'

Nurse Witch gripped the crutch so tightly, her fingers started to turn white. I had a horrible feeling she was trying to stop herself from hitting us with it. Ella had to hold on to the desk she was laughing so much.

'Her syndrome causes uncontrollable laughing too,' I said, which made Ella laugh even more.

I could feel Lucky starting to wriggle under my arm, and I knew I wasn't going to be able to hold her for much longer.

'Let's go,' I said. 'Gigi will be waiting.'

'Yip,' said Ella and Lucky together.

☽ ☺ ☼

'Where could Gigi be?' I asked when we got upstairs and found her room empty.

Then we heard the sound of laughing from the end of the corridor.

'The lounge,' said Ella. 'I forgot to tell you the residents are allowed to stay there until midnight these days.'

I followed her along the corridor and when we got to the lounge, it was like we were joining the best party in the world. Everyone was sitting around, chatting and laughing and listening to the radio that was playing in the corner. Hannah was knitting as usual, and Nancy was showing Fred old photographs from her tennis career.

'OMG – it's like a home,' I whispered to Ella. 'It's like a normal, happy home.'

Gigi looked up from her chat with Paddy. 'Girls!' she said. 'You're here at last. Would you like tea or coffee?'

We asked for tea, and while she went over to the fancy new machine in the corner of the room, I unwrapped Lucky, who blinked in the bright light of the room.

'Who gets first cuddle tonight?' I asked,

and backed away laughing as the old people shuffled towards me with their arms stretched out in front of them.

☺ ☺ ☼

Much later, Ella and I sat in the corner, watching as Lucky was passed around the room. Peggy was going from chair to chair, sharing a box of chocolates. Someone had switched off the radio, and Fred was singing a sad old song in a beautiful deep voice.

'This is so cool,' said Ella. 'Gigi is always going to miss her own home, but this is lovely too.'

'Yeah,' I said. 'I guess.'

'What?' asked Ella. 'What are you thinking?'

'It's *almost* perfect,' I said. 'But that's not good enough. Look how these people love Lucky. It's like hugging her is the best thing in their lives.'

'It's *one* of the best things,' said Ella. 'That's

why we risk bringing her in here every week.'

'Yeah, but don't you see the problem?'

'No.'

'Things can't go on like this. Someday we're going to get caught, and then we won't be able to bring Lucky here anymore. Once we're discovered, Nurse Witch will be watching out for her, and not even your best made-up-syndrome act will be able to fool her.'

'But if we're—'

'And it's not just about being caught,' I said. 'What about the times when you go away to visit your cousins? We won't be able to come here then. And next month, Maggie's going to visit Ruby for the weekend, and Lucky is going to stay with Ruby's uncle, so we won't be able to bring her that week either. Sneaking her in here is totally fun, but we both know it can't go on forever.'

'So what are we going to do?'

'Like I said before, we've got to get rid of

Nurse Witch.'

'But how? When I see her being mean I feel like pushing her down the stairs, but I'm not really a violent person, and anyway, I don't fancy spending twenty years in jail.'

'I've got an idea,' I said. 'We know Nurse Witch is terrified of animals, so how about we sneak in a cage full of rats and let them run around the place?'

'And you just happen to have a cage of rats lying around your house?'

'Not exactly – but we could use hamsters. Andy is always bragging about his collection of pedigree hamsters – why does everyone think he's so cool, by the way? Maybe he'd lend them to us for a day or two.'

'That would certainly get rid of Nurse Witch,' said Ella. 'But I'm guessing half the old people are afraid of rats and hamsters too. They could end up having heart attacks or something.'

'I suppose you're right,' I said. 'I never thought of that. We're going to have to think of something else.'

'Like what?'

'I know! Why don't we do what Peggy suggested? We could tell the local newspaper that this place is full of bed-bugs, and then Nurse Witch might get fired for running an unhygienic nursing home.'

Ella shook her head. 'If people think there are bed-bugs here, the whole place will be closed down and everyone will have to leave. That won't help us at all.'

'Why are you always so negative?' I asked, even though I knew she was right.

I wasn't mad at her, I was mad at myself. We needed a better plan, and no matter how hard I tried, I couldn't think of one.

☽ ☺ ☀

Ella and I decided it was best to sneak Lucky

out the front door when Nurse Witch wasn't looking, so we ended up lurking in the corridor near the reception desk as usual.

Ella rolled her eyes when we heard Nurse Witch on the phone.

'Might as well settle down,' she said. 'This could be a long one.'

'Oh, Mammy,' came the familiar voice from around the corner. 'Things have gone from bad to worse around here. The old people have ganged up on me and they are doing whatever they like. They're wandering around night and day, and ignoring all the rules I set up for their own safety. I dread coming in to work every morning.'

There was a silence, and I guess her mum was saying encouraging stuff to her.

'But I *can't* leave,' she said. 'I need the job. The mortgage isn't going to pay itself. Yes, Mammy, I know I should get another job, but where? I'm too old for the army now, and who wants a run-down old nurse who couldn't even manage a bunch of old people without causing a revolution? Yes, Mammy, I know what you always say. Every day, in every way, I'm getting better and better. Yes, Mammy. Night-night. See you next week.'

'OMG,' I whispered. 'That's it. We were looking at the problem the wrong way around. We don't have to scare Nurse Witch away from here. She already wants to leave. All we've got to do is find her a new job.'

'Oh, is that all?' asked Ella. 'That's easy then. I guess she'll be gone from here by tomorrow night.'

I punched her lightly on the arm. 'Very funny. Not. Now get ready to run. Nurse Witch is on the move.'

Chapter Twenty-three

§

'**W**hy exactly do you need *all* the newspapers?' asked the librarian next day.

'School project,' I said. I knew she'd get suspicious, so I gave her one of my best smiles.

Ella and I took the huge stack of newspapers to the big comfy chairs at the end of the room.

'Here,' I said, handing half of the papers to her. 'And don't get distracted by photos of cute babies.' (Ella has a thing about cute babies.) 'Go straight to the jobs pages and find something suitable for Nurse Witch.'

For a while, neither of us said anything as we flicked through the papers.

'OMG,' said Ella after a bit. 'Look at this. The local hospital is opening a new ward, and needs ten new nurses. Maybe that would suit Nurse Witch?'

I shook my head. 'That wouldn't be fair to sick people. Imagine waking up after an operation and seeing Nurse Witch standing over you with a needle and a pair of rubber gloves? You'd have an instant relapse.'

Ella giggled. 'I guess you're right. And I suppose that means she wouldn't be any good for this one – *matron needed for boarding school – must love children, and have a kind, caring attitude.*'

I laughed too. 'There's probably a reason Nurse Witch chose to join the army in the first place. Even though she's a nurse, I guess she figured out early that she doesn't have a kind or caring bone in her body.'

'Maybe she should have a complete change

of career?' said Ella. 'What about this one here – they're looking for a night watchperson at the old mill?'

'Let's see,' I said, leaning over so I could see better. 'Nurse Witch would be a great watchperson. One look at her and even the scariest criminals would run away screaming. She'd be so ... or maybe not. Look what it says at the end – *duties involve working with guard dogs.*'

Now we both laughed so much, the librarian glared at us over the top of her ugly red glasses.

'OMG,' said Ella. 'Can't you just imagine Nurse Witch huddled in a sentry box, with a big pack of German shepherds barking madly outside? I think I'd pay money to see that.'

After a bit we stopped laughing, and continued to flick through the newspapers. Soon I got distracted and started to wonder what it would be like to be grown up and looking for a job. All the ones here seemed kind of boring and time-consuming to me.

Who'd want to be an accountant or a lawyer?

What's fun about cleaning and ironing?

Why weren't there any ads for chocolate-tasters or trampoline testers?

And then Ella nudged me so hard, I let out a tiny squeak of pain.

'Sorry,' she said. 'I just got excited.'

'Why? Did you spot an incredibly cute baby?'

She rolled her eyes. 'No. I've found the perfect job for Nurse Witch.'

Without another word she handed the paper to me, and pointed at a big ad in the bottom corner.

Boot camp instructor urgently wanted. Knowledge of health and nutrition essential Tel 75-264-882 for immediate interview

'OMG!' I said. 'You genius! That's *exactly* the right job for Nurse Witch. It's totally perfect.

She'd actually get *paid* for being a bully. The more strict and horrible she is, the better they'll love her. There's no time to waste – we've got to make sure she applies before they give the job to someone else.'

I was already shoving the papers into an untidy pile. Ella stood up and helped me.

'Er ... how exactly are we going to get Nurse Witch to apply for this?'

'We photocopy the ad, put it in front of her, and cross our fingers.'

'You think that'll work?'

'Who knows? All we can do is try – and maybe we'd better cross our toes too – to be sure to be sure.'

☽　☺　☼

Ella keyed in the code, and we walked up to the reception desk. It felt kind of weird going in to the nursing home without Lucky under my arm. Nurse Witch stared at us.

'You two again!' she said. 'Haven't you got any homes to go to?'

'Of course we have,' I said, smiling sweetly. 'It's just that we like spending lots of time with old people. Who knows how long they've got to live, so we think it's important to be really, really nice to them.'

Nurse Witch sniffed. 'Well run along and try not to annoy the residents too much,' she said. 'I'm busy.'

She didn't look very busy. I leaned over the desk and saw the book she'd just put down. *Finding a new career – AT ANY AGE!*

I nudged Ella, and she remembered her part of the plan.

'Oh, look,' she said, pointing down the corridor. 'I think I see someone breaking a rule.'

While Nurse Witch turned and looked down the empty corridor, I slipped the photocopied page on top of her book.

'You're imagining things again, Ella.' I said. 'Now let's run up and say a quick hello to Gigi before it's time for our hockey practice.'

☽   ☺   ☼

When we came downstairs twenty minutes later, Nurse Witch was on the phone. Her hand was half-over the receiver, and her voice was weird – all fake and posh. She was speaking quietly, but we could still hear what she was saying – 'I'm calling about the advertisement in the newspaper – yes, I'm highly qualified – twenty years of nursing experience – an interview tomorrow at six? – Yes that sounds perfect.'

'Time for us to get out of here,' I said.

'Absolutely,' said Ella. 'We so don't want to be here when Nurse Witch starts to ask awkward questions about the sudden appearance of that ad on her desk.'

So we skipped and laughed our way out of

the nursing home like the bold kids Nurse Witch always thought we were.

Chapter Twenty-four

By the next Friday night, life in the nursing home was starting to change in a big way.

Gigi was cuddling Lucky when she told us the good news.

'Nurse Witch is leaving,' she said. 'She's got another job and she'll be gone by the end of next week.'

'That's totally amazing,' said Ella.

'What happened?' I asked, trying not to smile.

(Ella and I already had a fairly good idea of what had happened.)

'It's all very mysterious,' said Gigi. 'I

overheard Nurse Witch chatting to one of the care workers. She said that she found a piece of paper on her desk, and it had a job ad on it – an ad for an instructor at one of those boot camp places. I can't figure it out at all. How did that paper magically appear – with the ad all circled in bright red pen?'

I tried to look innocent. 'Who knows?' I said.

Gigi looked at Ella and me with a big twinkle in her eye. 'There's something you're not telling me, isn't there?'

'We might have got a *small* bit involved,' said Ella. 'And luckily it seems to have worked.'

And then I had a horrible thought. 'Maybe we didn't think this through properly,' I said. 'Who's going to replace Nurse Witch? And how can you be sure that the new matron won't be as bad as her, or maybe even worse?'

'*No one* could be as bad as Nurse Witch,' said Ella.

'You don't need to worry,' said Paddy wheeling himself over to join the conversation. 'The residents committee is going to be a big part of the selection process. Gigi and I are going to be on the interview panel, and I've already got my questions ready.'

'I like a man who's prepared for anything,' said Gigi, giggling like a little girl.

'OMG, Gigi!' said Ella looking horrified. 'Are you flirting?'

'Absolutely not,' said Gigi firmly, but when she turned away, I noticed that her cheeks had turned a pretty shade of pink.

Gigi was falling in love – how totally cute was that?

� ☺ ☼

Two weeks later, Ella and I walked up to the door of the nursing home.

'Come on,' I said to Lucky who was running along beside us. 'Time for your cuddling session.'

We let ourselves in and went up to the reception desk. Everything was different – and nicer. On the desk, there was a big bowl of jelly-beans. On the wall, where Nurse Witch's list of rules used to hang, there was a photograph of an old lady sky-diving. From the lounge, there came the sound of laughing and singing.

'Hello, Nurse Wilson,' said Ella, and the smiley lady shook her finger at us.

'Please call me Sylvie,' she said. 'Nurse Wilson makes me sound so old and starchy. Ella, I know you already, but who is your young friend?'

'My name's Eva,' I said.

'It's very nice to meet you, Eva,' said Sylvie as she came around to our side of the reception desk. 'And who is this darling, darling dog?' As she spoke, she bent down and picked Lucky up, and cuddled and kissed her.

'You're so sweet, I could eat you up with a spoon,' she said.

'Yip!' said Lucky, almost like she understood.

As Ella and I walked towards the stairs, I sniffed the air. 'What's that smell?' I said. 'It's almost like ...'

'Nail varnish,' said Ella. 'Sylvie has arranged for a nail artist to visit every two weeks.'

She pushed open the door to the downstairs lounge, and I could see a line of old people examining nail varnish samples, and holding out shaky old hands, all ready to be beautified.

'OMG!' I said to Ella as we went upstairs. 'I thought you were exaggerating, but you totally weren't. Sylvie is like an angel from a fairy-tale. Gigi and her friends must be so happy.'

'They are,' said Ella. 'They love Sylvie. Everything's perfect – except for one small thing.'

'What's that?'

'Gigi and her friends are all excited because I

said we were bringing Lucky to see them today. They've already drawn up a rota, deciding who will cuddle her, and for how long.'

'That's sweet,' I said. 'But I'm not seeing the problem here.'

'A few minutes once a week doesn't seem like enough time for the old people to spend with pets. I wish you and I had more time. I wish we could bring Lucky to visit every single day.'

I smiled and pulled a leaflet from my pocket. 'And that's why I've brought something to show them.'

‿ ☺ ☼

Gigi used the fancy new machine to make us hot chocolate, and then she went to the jar to get a handful of squishy marshmallows to put on top.

Ella sighed as she took the cup from her granny. 'I think I want to live here,' she said. 'Are teenagers allowed?'

'Now that Sylvie's here, who knows?' said Gigi. 'Anything could happen.'

'Anyway, girls, what news have you brought us from the outside world?'

I handed her the leaflet.

'My mum picked this up at the market the other day,' I said. 'And she immediately thought of you.'

Gigi took the leaflet and looked at it for a long time. Then she handed it to Paddy who read it and passed it on to Hannah.

'*Someone* rolled over my reading glasses in his wheelchair,' said Peggy, glaring at Paddy. 'So I can't see the leaflet properly. What's it about?'

I sat beside her and explained. 'It's about a group called "Pets for Good"' I said. 'It's run by volunteers who bring their pets to visit people in hospitals and nursing homes.'

'What do we want that for?' asked Peggy. 'We've got you and Lucky.'

'I'm glad you see it like that,' I said. 'But Ella and I have busy lives. We've got school and sport and hanging out to do. But these people could come every morning, and stay for an hour or two.'

'Would you and Ella still bring Lucky to see us?' asked Peggy.

'Of course we would,' I said. 'We'll still come any chance we get – but you'll love these pets too. They're specially chosen because they're really gentle and loving. And all you've got to do is persuade Sylvie that it's a good idea.'

'We're on it,' said Gigi jumping up and taking the leaflet from my hand. 'Come on, Paddy. This is a job for the residents association.'

'OMG!' said Ella, as soon as Gigi and Paddy had left. 'Did you see the way those two looked at each other? I think they might actually be dating, and I can't make up my mind if it's totally gross or totally sweet.'

'It's totally sweet,' I said. 'Your granny's got a boyfriend, Ella. Get over it.'

Chapter Twenty-five

It was Saturday, two weeks later.

'OMG, Eva,' said Ella. 'Where on earth did you get that dirty old jacket? You look a total mess.'

'Thanks a lot,' I said, pretending to be hurt. 'But we're supposed to be working. And anyway – you don't look so great yourself.'

She did a twirl so I could get a good view of her ancient old tracksuit and her flowery wellies.

'Enough with the fashion show,' I said laughing. 'We need to go. Everyone will be waiting.'

When we got to Maggie's place, Aretta and her dad were already there, along with a tall, skinny teenager who looked really like Aretta.

'Eva, Ella, at last you're here,' said Aretta, when she saw us. 'You've got to meet my brother, Damola. He's come to help us.'

Damola smiled at us and Aretta's dad put his arms around the two of them. 'My children are back together again,' he said.

'Are you moving here?' I asked Damola.

'Yes,' said Aretta firmly. 'His girlfriend's family are moving here next week, and Damola's coming too, aren't you?'

He shrugged. 'I quite like Dublin, but it doesn't look like I'm getting a choice, does it?'

'No,' said Aretta. 'It's sorted.'

☽   ☺   ☼

'What happened here?' asked Ella as we went around to the back of the house. 'It looks like a bomb landed and wiped everything out.'

'Dad and some of his friends have been coming here every evening after work,' I said. 'They've cleared everything and taken away all the old junk.'

'They have prepared a blank canvas for me,' said Aretta's dad, spreading his plan out on the patio. 'And I can't wait to get started on the new garden. I am so very excited about—'

Before he could finish, we heard the sound of Dad's rattly old van pulling up at the gate. We ran back outside and saw Dad's friend, Derek, jumping out of the van.

'Come on, you slackers,' he said. 'We've got work to do. Help me to unload this stuff.'

Dad had to do five trips to bring all the materials we needed. When we'd unloaded the fifth vanload, we took a break.

'Remind me again where all this stuff came from,' said Maggie as she handed out big glasses of lemonade.

'People are very generous,' said Dad.

'Sometimes all you have to do is ask. The scaffolding company donated all their old boards for the raised beds. The builders' provider supplied the cement and the nuts and bolts and things, and a contractor I know is delivering a load of topsoil this afternoon.'

'I don't see any plants,' said Ella. 'No offence, but all this stuff we've unloaded looks a bit grey.'

'Mum's bringing the plants later,' I said. 'Everyone in her garden club has donated something, so there's going to be heaps. When we're finished, Maggie's garden is going to be a jungle again – but in a good way.'

'Yip,' said Lucky, and everyone laughed.

☽ ☺ ☼

Mum woke me early on Sunday morning. 'Time to get up, Eva,' she said. 'We've got work to do.'

I groaned. 'Can't I take a day off?'

My back was still sore from the day before,

and I had blisters all over my hands from digging.

'It'll be worth the hard work when Maggie is able to use her garden again,' she said. 'And it's just a few more hours – Dad thinks we'll be finished by lunchtime.'

'OK, I get it,' I said. 'I'm up.'

I dragged myself out of bed and pulled on my dirty old working clothes.

Gardening, I said to myself. *I must put that on the list of jobs I don't want to do when I grow up.*

☽　☺　☼

It was a lovely sunny morning. There was no sign of Ella, but Dad set Aretta and me to work, painting the new gazebo he'd made out of the old shed. It was nice sitting there in the sunshine with my friend, watching as the faded grey wood disappeared under a coat of cool blue paint.

'Your dad looks so happy,' I said. 'It must be amazing to see his design coming to life.'

'He *is* happy,' said Aretta. 'He hasn't been this happy since we left Nigeria. And we got good news last night. My mother Skyped, and she thinks she has found a really nice sheltered home for her parents to live. It is just being built, but it will be ready next year. When my grandparents have settled in, my mother will be able to come here to live with us.'

'That's brilliant,' I said. 'I'm glad things are working out so well for you. I just hope ...'

'What?' asked Aretta.

'Well, I know your dad is totally happy now, but what's he going to do when Maggie's garden is finished? Is he going to go back to sitting in his room being sad and waiting for you to come home from school? I so hope that doesn't happen. You've got basketball to play, and Ella and I have got used to hanging around with you in the afternoons. And how will I ever manage maths without your help?'

Aretta smiled. 'You don't have to worry. I am going to have plenty of time for basketball and maths and hanging out and anything else I want to do.'

'Good to hear it,' I said. 'But how come?'

'The manager of the centre saw my father's plans for Maggie's garden, and he was really impressed. He asked my father to design a community garden for the waste space behind the centre. Dad's already got heaps of ideas. It's going to be really cool, with swings for the kids, and vegetable gardens and flowers and everything.'

'And who's going to build it?' I asked.

'That's the great thing,' said Aretta. 'The manager said he will provide the materials, if my father and the other residents will do the work. Everyone's really enthusiastic, and there's a great atmosphere in the centre these days.'

Just then Ella showed up. 'You're late,' I said.

'What time do you think ...?'

But I stopped talking when I saw her face.

'Hey,' I said, dropping my paintbrush and rushing over to her. 'What's wrong?'

'I went to see Gigi this morning,' she said. 'And she had very sad news. Hannah died during the night.'

I felt tears come to my eyes as I remembered the sweet old lady who was always knitting.

I remembered how bravely she had stood up to Nurse Witch.

It was cold the last time I'd seen her, and she'd rubbed my icy fingers and promised to knit me a pair of warm gloves.

'That's so sad,' I said. 'Poor Hannah.'

'Her son was there this morning,' said Ella. 'And Gigi introduced us. He asked me if I was one of the girls with the dog, and when I told him I was, he gave me a huge hug. "Mam told me all about you and your friend," he said. 'On my last visit, all she talked about was how much she enjoyed your Friday night visits. You made Mam's last days on earth so happy, and we will always be grateful for that.'

'That's so sweet,' I said.

'And it gets better,' said Ella. 'Hannah's son said she had left some money to the nursing home and Sylvie want to use it to make a garden where the residents can sit on sunny days.'

'Cool,' I said.

I had a weird feeling of being sad and happy, all mixed up together. I hated the idea of never seeing Hannah again, but it was nice to know how much she'd enjoyed our visits with Lucky. It was nice to know that, because of Hannah, the nursing home residents would get a lovely garden to hang out in.

'And there's more good news,' said Ella. 'Sylvie has given the OK to the Pets for Good scheme, and they're going to start visiting next week. One man is going to bring his pet alpaca.'

'OMG,' I said. 'That's the best and craziest thing I've ever heard.'

'There's still more,' said Ella.

I grinned. 'I'm not sure if I can stand the excitement.'

'Sylvie says that as soon as the garden is ready, she'd like to get a dog to live at the nursing home. We're hoping that dog might be Pedro.'

'This is like a fairy-tale.' I said, 'Everything's working out so well.'

Aretta came over and we told her all the news.

'I think my father would like to help with the garden design for the nursing home,' she said. 'He would know all the things to do to make it suitable for old people.'

'Are you sure?' I said. 'I know he's great and all that, but is it fair to ask him to do all that work when he can't even get paid for it?'

Aretta's dad came over and heard what I said. 'Being paid would be good,' he said. 'I would like to buy nice things for my children – but that is not possible right now, so, for the moment, I am happy to help with worthy projects.'

Aretta put her arm around him. 'That's my father,' she said proudly. 'And when our asylum is granted, people will be queuing up to give him work. He will be the most famous garden designer in the whole country.'

And I had a funny feeling she was right.

Half way through the afternoon, the work was finally finished. I stood up from where I'd been planting small blue flowers, wondering if I'd ever be able to straighten my back properly again.

'Thank you all so much,' said Maggie. 'I now have the most beautiful garden in Ireland. My brother is on his way over to tidy up the last few pieces, and while he's doing that, I would like you all to go home and wash and change.'

'You saying we're dirty?' I said, stepping forward so everyone could see my clothes that were covered in blue paint, cement and general mucky stuff.

'Whatever,' said Maggie. 'Anyway, everyone is to take an hour off, and please come back at five o'clock for the official opening of my wonderful new garden.'

Chapter Twenty-six

When Mum and Dad and Ella and I got back to Maggie's place at five, there was an incredible smell of flowers and baking and barbecued meat all mixed up together.

Maggie met us at the front door. 'I prepared some food,' she said. 'I had to try out my new barbecue. Now why don't you all come in?'

Aretta and her brother and dad were in the kitchen with Dad's friend Derek, and a few of Mum's friends from the gardening club. Everyone was staring at me, and smiling like crazy.

'What's going on?' I asked Ella. 'Have I got

blue paint on my face or something?'

But she just smiled too.

'Let's go outside,' said Maggie. 'I'll lead the way – now that I can.'

We all followed her outside. Now that everything had been swept and tidied, the garden looked totally amazing. Maggie wheeled her chair up and down the new wide paths. She showed us how she could pull weeds out of the raised beds, and how she could use the special pulley-things Aretta's dad had made, so she could lower and raise the hanging baskets whenever she needed to plant or water them.

'It's perfect,' said my mum. 'Absolutely perfect.'

Everyone agreed, and there were lots of handshakes and pats on the back for Aretta's dad, who looked totally embarrassed.

'Oh, dear,' said Maggie then. 'My wheels seem to be squeaking again. Does anyone know where the oil is?'

'I put it in the storage area behind the gazebo,' said Aretta's dad.

'Oh, Eva,' said Maggie. 'Would you mind getting it for me, please?'

Suddenly I felt cross. The whole idea of the makeover was so that Maggie could access every corner of the garden, and now, on the very first day, she was asking me to get stuff for her.

Why couldn't she act a bit more grateful? Was all the hard work for nothing?

'Maybe *you* should—' I began, but Mum interrupted.

'Don't argue, Eva,' she said. 'Just do it.'

'But—'

'*Eva!*' said Dad. Now I really felt like arguing, but I didn't like the way everyone was staring at me, with funny, smiley looks on their faces.

Were they laughing at me?

How dare they laugh at me?

I stamped down the garden and as soon as I got to the end – 'Surprise!'

I jumped back, half-scared, as three girls jumped out from where they were hiding behind the gazebo.

'OMG!' I said, hardly able to believe my eyes. 'Kate? Victoria? Ruby?'

And then I couldn't say any more as they all jumped on top of me and hugged me until I begged for mercy.

Finally we untangled ourselves, and Ella and Aretta came to join us.

'Did you two know about this?' I asked.

'Sort of,' said Ella grinning.

'So what happened?' I asked. 'Why are you all here?'

'Well,' said Ruby. 'It's my mid-term break, and Mum was going to come to London to visit me, but when you came up with the garden idea, we swapped the tickets around, so I could come here and surprise you instead. This whole party is Mum's way of saying thanks to you for getting the garden done up.'

'And I haven't seen you for ages and ages,' said Kate. 'And I was dying to meet your new friend, so when your mum rang me up and invited me, it was a no-brainer.'

'And what about you?' I asked Victoria.

'If Kate and Ruby were coming halfway around the world to see you, of course I'd come from the other side of town.'

Suddenly I noticed that Aretta was standing on her own at the edge of the group.

'Hey, Aretta,' I said. 'This is everyone. Everyone this is Aretta, the maths genius.' Aretta looked embarrassed. 'I'm serious,' I said. 'Since you started helping me, maths actually makes sense, and you can't believe what a big deal that is. I got a B in my last test, which is like a million times better than I've ever done before. I owe you, Aretta.'

She pointed at her dad, who was talking to my mum and dad. He had his arm around Damola, and he had a huge, happy smile on his face.

'I think we might be quits,' she said quietly.

'Food's ready,' called Maggie from the barbeque corner, and my friends and I went over with our plates and the best party ever got started.

The 'Eva' Series
by
Judi Curtin

Don't miss the other great books about Eva
and her friends

Have you read them all?

Eva's Journey

Eva's Holiday

Leave it to Eva

Eva and the Hidden Diary

Available from all good bookshops.

Eva Gordon is a bit of a princess ...

But when her dad loses his job and she has to move house and change schools, she realises things have changed forever. A chance visit to a fortune teller gives her the idea that doing good may help her to turn things back the way they were. Eva (with the help of best friend Victoria) starts to help everyone she can — whether they want it or not! And maybe being nice is helping Eva herself just as much ...

The story of
Eva's marvellous,
memorable summer!

Eva Gordon likes fashion, fun and hanging out with friends,
so she can't believe she has to spend the entire summer in a
cottage in the countryside with her parents.

Worse, it looks like she's going to be stuck with Kate, the
girl next door who doesn't care about being cool ... But when
the girls have to pull together to solve a problem, Eva finds out
that there's more to life than having the right hair or clothes
and sometimes 'weird' girls can make the best friends.

Fun, feisty Eva Gordon
always tries to help
her friends!

When Eva and her family head to Seacove for their summer holidays, she's
looking forward to seeing Kate again, but it turns out things have gone very
wrong for Kate. Her granny's in the hospital, and with no else to look after
her, Kate's hiding out at home by herself, afraid she's going to be taken into
care. Eva tries to be a good friend and help her out, but how long can
a twelve-year-old manage by herself?

It's not just Kate who needs Eva's help — and helping Ruby turns out
to be a LOT of fun!

Eva Gordon's great at solving problems, but surely even she can't fix something that went wrong in the past?

When Eva and Kate find an old diary, written long ago by a girl their own age, they end up determined to right old wrongs!

But they can't spend all their time living in the past as the present, too, is throwing all sorts of challenges at them ...

THE 'ALICE & MEGAN' SERIES
BY

HAVE YOU READ THEM ALL?

Don't miss all the great books about Alice & Megan:

Alice Next Door
Alice Again
Don't Ask Alice
Alice in the Middle
Bonjour Alice
Alice & Megan Forever
Alice to the Rescue
Alice & Megan's Cookbook
Viva Alice
Available from all good bookshops

www.judicurtin.com

BONJOUR ALICE

ALICE & MEGAN FOREVER

ALICE TO THE RESCUE

VIVA ALICE!

www.judicurtin.com